THE SEARCH

THE SEARCH

by

IAIN CRICHTON SMITH

LONDON
VICTOR GOLLANCZ LTD
1983

© Iain Crichton Smith 1983

British Library Cataloguing in Publication Data
Smith, Iain Crichton
The search.
I. Title
823'.914[F]   PR6005.R58

ISBN 0–575–03297–9

Typeset by Colset Pte Ltd, Singapore
Printed in Great Britain by St Edmundsbury Press, Bury St Edmunds, Suffolk

THE SEARCH

One

SITTING IN HIS Spartan room in the college in Canberra
Trevor heard the phone ring. He picked it up and a voice said,

"You won't know me but I was listening to your interview on local radio and I thought, 'Your name is Grierson
and you come from Scotland.' I wonder if by any chance you
have a brother in Australia. Are you listening? It seemed to
me that your accent was the same as his. Are you there, Mr
Grierson?"

Trevor heard the voice coming to him as it were from
outer space, as if some trick were being played on him, and
the room was suddenly populated with images from his
childhood and youth.

"Yes," he said at last, "I have a brother in Australia. I
haven't heard from him for years."

"Well, then," said the voice, which seemed to be far and
near at the same time. "I think there is something I should
tell you. May I come and see you?"

"Yes," said Trevor, "if you have news of him come and
see me. I'll make a point of staying in. Do you want to come
now?"

"Well . . ." said the voice hesitantly.

"Order a taxi, I'll pay for it. Come right away."

"No, that's all right. I'll take the bus," said the voice, this time decisively.

Trevor put the phone down and sat staring into space. In that moment it was as if the college in which he was living had disappeared with all its fine rooms, its paintings, the pond in which the goldfish cruised in a leisurely manner, the wine which he drank with the lecturers, the common room in which the books and newspapers were. His brother? But he hadn't heard from him for twenty years. What had happened in the interval? What was wrong with him? Was he dead? The voice had sounded both ominous and gentle, as if it were the bearer of bad news. He pushed the phone away from him and from an obscure impulse put back into the cupboard the glass with the whisky from which he had been drinking. It was as if he found the luxury repulsive and was glad when the room became austere again with its table and two chairs, cupboard and wooden folding partition which hid the kitchenette from sight. What would this man have to tell him about his brother? Was it fated that he himself should have come to Australia at this precise time?

The picture of his brother which hung on the wall of his house back in Glasgow appeared in front of his eyes. The cap of the Scottish regiment was tilted slightly and rather rakishly over the right eye, the shirt was green and open-necked, the expression clear and unclouded.

At the age of 21, shortly after he had finished his National Service, his brother had set off to Australia and they had all, himself, his mother and Sheila, seen him off. Norman had waved cheerfully from the railing of the ship and it was as if he was setting off on some tremendous adventure, fresh and young. He had written for a while and then they had heard nothing from him. His mother had died without knowing where he was, and indeed ignorant whether he was still alive or not. And now there was only Trevor himself and his wife, Sheila, who was back in Scotland. Trevor was a lecturer in English in Glasgow University, now for a brief while in Canberra University lecturing on Scottish writers, especially Robert Louis Stevenson.

Suddenly he went over to the cupboard again and took another whisky. It seemed so odd that his caller should have sprung immediately to the conclusion that he was related to Norman. Was he some sort of crank? But if he was, he had at least been right in his conclusion. He waited for the step on the stair as if his fate were to be decided. In a strange sort of way he felt it unjust that that voice should have interrupted him at that moment in his life, as if some malevolent being in the sky were playing a trick on him. He was quite conscious of the difference between his own circumstances and those in which he feared his brother might be living. Most of the time since he had arrived in Canberra he had spent listening to lectures, or himself lecturing, drinking wine, discussing literature in a civilized manner with men who had never known insecurity or failure. His surroundings, too, could not have been more pleasant. His room, though austere, was comfortable, the campus was beautiful with trees in a fury of autumn colours, there was a library available and in general he was living in luxury and opulence under a sky of unvarying blue.

At last he heard footsteps on the stair and at first thought they might be those of the Japanese physicist who stayed opposite him on the same landing. But, no, they were coming straight for his door. There was a knock and he opened the door immediately. A dark-haired, sturdy man came into

11

the room; he was wearing a blue jacket and a shirt which was open at the neck.

"My name's Douglas," he said. "Malcolm Douglas. I am the person who phoned you."

"Oh," said Trevor, and then, almost foolishly, "Would you like a drink?"

"No, thanks," said Douglas who was looking around the room as if trying to memorize it. For some reason known only to himself he was smiling. Almost as if he were laughing at me, thought Trevor. That's very odd.

"Well," said Trevor, leaning urgently forward. "What have you to tell me?"

"Norman used to talk a lot about you," said Douglas. "He said you worked in Glasgow University. Is that right?"

"Yes," said Trevor, "that's where I work." Through the window he could see the eucalyptus trees shedding their bark, white and ghostly, and once he saw a cockatoo with green exotic plumage flying from one branch to another.

"Did he tell you much about me?" Trevor said.

Without answering his question, Douglas said, "I'd better come straight to the point. Your brother's dead, you know."

Again it was as if Trevor sensed a bitter laughter rippling behind the blunt statement. And the tears welled to his eyes. His brother couldn't be dead. Not Norman who had set off so hopefully and eagerly to this land of the young. Not Norman who had been so full of life. Why, when he had first arrived in Australia he had ridden on a horse throughout the country. Or so he had written in one of his occasional brief letters. His mind sheered away from the dark fact of his death as if it were an obstacle that had reared up suddenly and blankly in front of that pirouetting horse.

12

"I'm sorry," said Douglas, "but it's better to tell you. You haven't heard from him for a long time, have you? Right?"

"That's true," said Trevor, still thinking of the photograph which hung on the wall and which he had insisted that Sheila leave there.

"The last I heard of him," said Douglas, "was that he had died in the cells in Sydney."

"Cells?" said Trevor faintly. "I don't understand."

"That's right. A Pole told me. Mind you, I don't know how far these Poles can be trusted. Some of them tell the most awful lies. God knows why they do it: perhaps to draw attention to themselves." He took out some tobacco and began to roll a cigarette.

"Have one of mine," said Trevor, throwing him a full packet. "I got them on the plane."

"Thanks. As I was saying, one doesn't know why they say these things, but they do. This Pole told someone I know that your brother had died in the cells in Sydney."

Oh my God, thought Trevor, they have beaten him up. I have read stories like that in the newspapers. They have beaten him to death with their batons so far from home. I can't stand it.

Douglas gazed at him from behind a wreath of cigarette smoke with an infuriating blandness.

"I got out of that life in time, myself. I'm married now. But I was like that, too. I stayed in lodging houses and homes. Norman . . ." He paused. "Well, one night, he was walking along the street with a brick in his hand. He was going to break in somewhere, a warehouse, I think it was. I imagine he was drunk out of his mind; and the police got him. Loitering with intent, I suppose you could call it." He

13

leaned forward and stubbed out the cigarette in the blue ashtray which was lying on the table.

"This can't be true," thought Trevor. "I don't believe this nightmare. Norman was never like that."

"Norman . . ." he began.

Douglas smiled as if he were talking to a child and said, "When did you see him last, as a matter of interest?"

"Eighteen years ago," said Trevor hopelessly.

"There you are then. He's changed a lot since then. You wouldn't recognize him now. He used to talk about his mother a lot. Is she dead?"

"Yes."

"Uh, huh. Anyway that was what the Pole told one of my mates, that he had died in a cell. I heard your voice on the radio and I recognized the accent. Norman used to talk exactly like that."

"Are you absolutely sure he's dead?" said Trevor desperately. "Maybe I could find him and bring him . . ."

"Home?" Douglas sounded suddenly aggressive. "Tell me, Mr Grierson, have you thought where his home is now? And what exactly are you implying? When I came back into circulation again my sister wouldn't speak to me. She thinks of me as the black sheep of the family. Were you going to offer him money? I told you Norman has changed. Even if he's alive he won't go home, not on your terms. Are you patronizing him? Why do you want him home anyway?"

Trevor became suddenly angry in his turn.

"I know why I want him home," he said.

"Why?"

"Because he's poor. Because he doesn't have any money. I have gathered that from what you said. That's why I would bring him home."

"Norman drinks a lot, Mr Grierson. Did you know that if you are an alcoholic you may not adjust to another country. And in any case you can't just go to your brother and say to him, 'Come home at once.' Think about it. Are you doing it because you want your conscience set at rest, not that I'm saying that you have anything to be sorry for. Do you understand me?"

Trevor considered for a moment and then he said, though he was still angry, "I can see what you're getting at but I'm not a fool. I can recognize my own motives and take account of them."

"That may be your opinion, Mr Grierson." And then, quite inconsequentially, Douglas proceeded, "What do you think I live on, myself, my wife and child. We live on seventy dollars a week. That's thirty-five pounds in your money. I'm unemployed. It's not that I can't get a job but I can't get one I like."

His face twitched for a moment and then he said, "I'm sorry. I get these headaches. I was typing till late last night. I'm writing a book."

"A book?"

"A book based on my experiences. Do you think someone like me can't write a book? I met this man, a homosexual, and he told me that he had killed three little girls. It was all in the papers, a big unsolved crime. I said to myself, 'It's nothing to do with me. Why should I help the police? They've done nothing for me.' And so I didn't do anything about it. Then a week after that I saw another girl had been killed. I went to the police and they showed me a lot of photographs. I pointed to one of them and they said, 'It can't be him. We've got another suspect in mind.' That was the first time I went."

"And the second time?"

"They believed me but they wanted to pin something on me, too. I felt as if I was the criminal. I don't like talking to the police. Norman was in the hands of the police, you know. If you're nothing and nobody how do you think they treat you?"

In his mind's eye Trevor saw the goldfish swimming restlessly about the pond in the courtyard of the college. He saw the arid lawns on which the sprinklers rotated without cease, and he gritted his teeth.

The remorseless voice continued, "I'm writing a novel based on that and my other experiences."

Trevor suddenly thought, "That's why he came. He hoped I would read his manuscript for him and perhaps find him a publisher."

"No, it isn't that," said Douglas, as if he had sensed what Trevor was thinking, "It's not because of the manuscript I came to see you. My book will do well anyway." And he became aggressive again, a nerve twitching in his cheek. "There are a lot of authors who allow middlemen to get the money they should have, but I'll set my own price for my work. Every word in that book is authentic. I've got a man in Hollywood reading it at the moment. It's interesting the contacts you make."

He lit another Marlborough from the pack Trevor had given him.

"I don't know whether that Pole was telling the truth or not. On the other hand, Norman is no fool. He read a lot of books, you know."

It was as if a warning bell rang in Trevor's mind.

"Books?" he asked. "What books?"

16

"Oh, books about philosophy and subjects like that."

No that couldn't be Norman, Trevor thought. Norman had never read books in his whole life: he had hated school and when he had finally left it nobody could have been happier. It was only with great difficulty that he had been forced to attend school and even then he often played truant, after his mother had left him at the gate.

"Are you sure about that?" said Trevor.

"Of course I'm sure. I loaned him some books myself. I told you Norman has changed. He's not the same boy you knew. Norman has worked out a way of surviving."

Surviving? But surely he had told him that he was dead.

"Norman's tougher than you think. He was also in New Zealand; did you know that? I was with him and two other fellows one night in a poolroom and he told them that he could speak Maori. And he could too. He spoke it to them. He said he could speak English and Maori: these were his two languages. Norman was a smart boy. Listen, for all I know that Pole may have been lying. Some of them do that to impress you. Would you believe that? That's what they like to do. I've never yet met a Pole who wasn't a liar. They love to lie and tell stories. But this Pole said that he had been staying with Norman in the same rooming house. I used to stay there myself. It was called the Michael Tranter."

Trevor thought for a moment and then said, "Surely I could phone that place and find out if Norman is still there?"

"You could do that. But there's another thing. He might have changed his name, given the wrong name. You never know."

"Changed his name?"

"Why not? He might. He did use to work but the last

17

time I saw him he wasn't working.''

"But wouldn't he need his right name for Social Security?''

"He might.'' Again Trevor felt the laughter rippling underneath the man's words. He was beginning to wonder whether his visitor was not a psychopath, an essentially malicious man who, hearing him speak on the radio, was determined to uproot him from his sheltered world. And yet he had known that his brother's name was Norman. Or was it he himself who had introduced the name? He couldn't remember.

"What else do you know about him?'' he asked.

"About Norman?'' Douglas blew smoke away from his mouth and considered. "He said that he had been sailing for a while and that he had been in the Army. He was serving in the Argylls, wasn't he, during his National Service. Isn't that right?''

"I don't know about the sailing. But he was certainly in the Army. Where could he have been sailing?''

"Well, he might have been sailing since he came out here. Or he might just have made that up. A lot of them make up stories, you know. I did meet Norman, you don't have to be so suspicious. He was a very kind and unhappy boy. We stayed in the same room together. And not a very nice room either.''

He stubbed out his cigarette and lit another.

"He may not be dead. It's possible that he might be still alive. As I say, you get all sorts of rumours.''

"Well, then,'' said Trevor, "well, then.'' He knew that he should ask more questions but he couldn't think of any. And in the middle of his indecision he saw Douglas rising to his feet, and he heard him say,

18

"I'd better leave you then. I thought you ought to be told of his death."

"What does he look like? Have you any photographs?" Trevor asked desperately.

"No, I'm afraid I haven't. We weren't in the business of taking photographs. You probably wouldn't recognize him now." Douglas spoke so casually that Trevor felt like hitting him: it was after all his brother he was talking about.

However he said, calmly enough, "I'll give you money for a taxi. Are you staying far from here?"

"It's all right," said Douglas, "I'll get a bus."

"But it's a Sunday," said Trevor. "Are you sure you'll get a bus?"

"No worries. I'll get a bus. Glad to have met you. Let me know what happens. Are you thinking of going to Sydney?"

"I'll have to, won't I? Since that's where you met him."

"Good luck then. Let me know what happens," said Douglas again.

"What's your phone number then?" Trevor asked.

Douglas hesitated for what seemed like quite a long time and then gave a phone number which Trevor wrote in his address book after his visitor's name.

Douglas then left.

After he had gone Trevor sat in his chair in a daze. Was it Norman the two of them had been talking about? Perhaps it had all been a case of mistaken identity. In any case, what could he do? What was the best thing? He went to the cupboard and drank a huge whisky at a gulp. As he did so, he thought, "I'd better not go the way my brother went." And then as he rehearsed Douglas's story in his mind he noticed some peculiarities. First of all his brother had never read books, and the second odd thing was about the sailing.

19

When and where had he done any sailing? Not unless he had done some round the Australian coast. On the other hand it was definitely true that he had served in the Army and had worn the diced cap of the Argylls. But perhaps this man Douglas had some twisted motive for what he was doing. Had he come to see him about his brother's presumed death in order to upset him? Was the Pole whom he kept mentioning a complete fabrication? Was Douglas a sadist of some sort? And what about the book he was writing? The whole tale seemed very odd. And what could he himself do even if he did go to Sydney? Lighting a cigarette he began to think; and as he was doing so he suddenly felt intense panic. He went to the door and turned the key in the lock of the main door and also in that of the door which led on to the balcony. Through its glass panes he could see the cockatoos flying about the naked trees. He felt bare and vulnerable in the world like a new-born bird. It was as if a breeze, heavy with deadly odour, had blown in on him from another world which travelled darkly beside the world he knew: everything looked fragile and unguarded. The gravity of that other secondary world — or perhaps it had been the real world all the time — was sucking him in. He picked up the phone and dialled the bus station.

'Do you have a bus going to Sydney?'' he asked.

Yes, they had; it left at five o'clock in the evening.

Two

IN THE MORNING he rang up Professor Hastie at the university to say that he wouldn't be able to come in that day as he had some pressing business to attend to in Sydney. In the light of morning he felt as if the conversation of the night before had never happened. He began to think of Douglas as some kind of madman who had decided to play a malignant trick on him because he was in comfortable circumstances and in an alien land. Professor Hastie's civilized voice soothed him.

"Of course," he said. "No worries. Take as long as you like."

At that moment Trevor nearly told him what he was going to Sydney for but decided against it. Strange speculations absorbed him. What if Douglas followed him to Sydney? What if he was stalking his brother for some perverse reason of his own and was using Trevor in order to find him?

These ideas preoccupied him even when he was in the Tourist Bureau fixing up accommodation. He was told of a hotel called the Australian which was not too expensive, and which, on Elizabeth Street, was fairly central: they had sent many customers there before and had had no complaints so far. Of course at this time of year accommodation was scarce. Trevor only half-listened, thinking of the journey ahead of him. Maybe, though Douglas himself might not be on the bus, he might send someone in his place. Hadn't he said that he had been in jail at least once, or was that something that Trevor had picked up wrong? In a peculiar way, whenever he thought of the conversation of the previous night, he felt as if it had all been an illusion, a trick. The odd, almost mocking smile returned to him.

As he walked restlessly about Canberra, killing time till the bus left, he found himself thinking that he might not be able to come back there if he left. The clean city with its towering offices and tidy shopping precincts seemed suddenly protected and ordinary. Once however he found himself staring at a young, long-haired, bare-footed hippy who was playing a guitar outside a jeweller's shop in the opulent precinct, while beside him on the pavement was a cap with some coins in it. In another part of the precinct a crowd had gathered round a man who was standing on a wooden stage and giving reasons in a loud voice why Australia should send its athletes to the Olympics. He remembered vaguely reading something in a paper about some trouble to do with the Olympics but couldn't recall exactly what it had been.

For most of the day he sat on a bench reading a book, watching the people passing, and once staring for what seemed to be hours at a little bird that was busily pecking at crumbs that were lying on the stone. Around him the bland, timeless Australian sunlight shone.

Once it occurred to him that he should phone Sheila, but eventually he decided against it. There was no point in worrying her; and as yet he had no real information about Norman. As he sat there he couldn't help comparing littered Glasgow with this hygienic city with its clean streets and restaurants.

At twenty minutes to five he was at the bus station with his case. He recalled that as he had left the college he had the strangest feeling that he would never see it again, that he was entering a world from which, even if he did return, it would be as someone who was irretrievably wounded. It was as though a shadow had fallen across the lawn, as if the birds that flew so colourfully among the trees were a mockery of his own life. He was reminded of the manic laughter of the kookaburra which he heard at dawn among the flutey, watery voices of other, but nameless, birds. Indeed at the moment he had left, someone had been playing a flute and he had listened to the notes as if they were saying goodbye to him and to the world in which he had hitherto lived.

As he sat in the station waiting for the bus to leave he looked around him at the other people who were waiting. None of them seemed to belong to the world that Douglas had talked of. There were four girls who, he thought, were Malaysian, and they were giggling like children over some joke or secret of their own. There was an old man and his wife, both with sunburnt, wrinkled faces, and obviously from the United States, for the man was wearing the sort of white hat that Americans wear. There was a young man sitting quietly by himself, and a very old woman with a ravaged face who was wearing a very short skirt which would have been more suitable on a teenager. By the number of labels on her cases she seemed to have travelled widely. There was also a Jap and his wife, both young, the former now and again consulting a huge complicated-looking watch at frequent intervals. No, there didn't seem to be anyone belonging to Douglas's world here, he was pretty sure of that. They all appeared to be simple, sincere tourists, many of them with brochures in their hands.

When the bus finally arrived and he climbed the steps he found that it was very cool, with perspex windows which made the world outside appear blue. He had been assigned a seat at the back next to the window and as he sat there he began to think what he should do in Sydney. The most obvious move was to call at the offices of Births, Marriages and Deaths, and ask if his brother was listed among the dead. As he thought of his morbid journey he felt both anger and sadness, anger because his smooth life was being upset and sadness because his brother might after all be dead. He remembered the two of them as they had been when they were quite young, often fighting as brothers do, but in emergencies combining against outsiders. There was, in particular, the day when he himself, then perhaps nine, had deliberately lost Norman in the woods and the latter had come home to their mother in tears accusing Trevor of having tormented him. His mother had asked Trevor that day,

"Why do you do these things? Are you jealous of him or what?"

In school he had of course been much cleverer than Norman, effortlessly winning prizes, making his easy way to university. But, when he came to think of it, his brother had been physically much stronger than him, a hard, tough fighter, completely fearless. He had once ridden home on his motorbike through a thunderstorm of frightening intensity, blue theatrical lightning at the tips of his gloves: yet though drenched he had been unafraid.

How odd it was that in the unfolding diary of his mind he could find so little in common between them. He himself had never been as adventurous as his brother nor so instinctively generous and hot-tempered. And of course their jobs had been very different. While he himself had been in university Norman had worked in a clock-making factory, coming back home in his overalls. Some nights he would be drunk and often aggressive while he himself was preparing his lecture notes. Norman's cheerful, yet sometimes vicious, face, glowed in the gathering darkness, as the bus raced towards Sydney. As Trevor looked out of the window he could see the brown parched land, dry as a bone, from which the light was fading, and it seemed to correspond to some inner landscape deep in his own nature.

Once he saw a crow pecking out the eyes of a lamb while the exhausted mother looked on helplessly, but most of the time there was only monotonous landscape over which no rain had fallen since he had come to Australia seven weeks before. He could see cattle resting on their shadows in the blue light and later a man riding a horse. As the darkness thickened the lights of small farmhouses glimmered in the distance.

The phrase "Am I my brother's keeper?" swam into his mind without bidding. Norman had liked his period of National Service, had enjoyed the comradeship and adventure. He himself had never done National Service because he had been continually deferred and later they had found that his eyes were weak. It had never occurred to him to ask Norman much about that period in his life. In fact when he came to think about it he didn't know much about Norman from the time that he had left home to join the Army or what events there had made him so restless later. How could this have happened? And yet when he had heard of his death, or presumed death, the tears had sprung to his eyes. It was lucky that their mother was no longer alive or the revelations, if true, would have shamed her. And yet he couldn't imagine that his brother would have been in trouble with the police, and least of all could he imagine that he would ever have stolen anything. Sheila, of course, hadn't wanted to get in touch with him. He should have been more insistent than he had been.

Sheila. . . . He blinked and turned his eyes again on the dim landscape through which the bus was travelling. The last light had drained out of it. Now and again a truck lit up like a Christmas tree with red lights loomed in front of the bus and then disappeared. They passed through the empty streets of small towns whose shops were illuminated and shut: launderamas, jewellers, petrol stations with their flags. And then they were out of the towns and on to the open road with the flicker of farm lights well away from the road.

He glanced to his right and saw that the old woman with the short skirt was asleep, her mouth open and slack. For some reason she reminded him of his mother and he imagined her trailing his brother through Australia with a Bible in her hand. Her voice came back to him across the years, "Make sure that you put on your tie, and comb your hair." He and his brother were setting off to school in the early morning, the berries shining redly on the trees among the heat haze, while they swung their schoolbags carelessly. The other boys were shouting "Sissy" and "Swot" after him and Norman was grim-faced and angry, as if ashamed of him.

He calculated, glancing at his watch, that they would reach Sydney at about ten o'clock. The driver had taken to using his microphone and was telling them a little of the dark country through which they were passing, and about the small town where they were to stop for refreshments. Trevor heard a woman with an Irish accent saying, "I prefer Melbourne. My daughter lives there. Do you know Melbourne?" Another bus passed them going in the same direction and the driver said,

"I beat him last week so this week he's trying to beat me." Another huge truck loomed out of the darkness, and then was gone. What was he doing on this road so far from home? He felt himself engaged on a rescue operation which at the same time appeared absurd. He thought of himself rushing into a room and saying to his wounded brother, "I have come to fetch you home. I have come to save you." But what would Sheila have to say about that? And would his brother be able to get a job when he came home? No, that wasn't the important thing. The important thing was to find him.

All the time that he had been lecturing on Robert Louis Stevenson that other world, of deprivation and despair, had been in existence, dark and enigmatic. How had he managed to evade it? Simply by winning the rewards that he had won. In the gathering darkness he saw the bare-footed guitarist playing for money while no one listened to him. Men were beaten up in parks, in police stations, beggars walked the streets.

Your brother has changed, Douglas had said. He had even taken to reading books. What if he passed him and didn't even recognize him? What if the man Douglas was talking about wasn't his brother at all? He felt badly in need of advice, of the opinion of an outsider. This burden which had been placed on his shoulders seemed too heavy for him. On the other hand he had been used to burdens, he had looked after his parents in their old age. And there was many a time

27

when he had cursed his brother who had vanished so conveniently into the blue when he had needed him, not even sending a Christmas card home. Not even a present to his mother. He had eeled so easily out of his responsibilities as if sliding out of his overalls when coming home from work.

And to tell the truth he felt frightened. What was this huge city Sydney like? What would he find in the office to which he was heading like a missile through the night among all these sleeping people, with their heads lolling back on seats? Even if he found that Norman was dead he would have to discover whether he had been given a proper burial. He might even have had a pauper's funeral, interred hugger mugger somewhere. But the worst thought was that he might not be able to find him at all and he would forever after wonder what had happened to him.

The old woman sat up with a jolt and smiled at him. The girl sitting in front of him went on remorselessly reading her book. The Malaysian girls were giggling secretly together in the hooded light.

Why hadn't Douglas kept in touch with his brother all those years if he had been so interested in him? Why had he so suddenly and brutally told him of a death which wasn't even definite but had been accepted on hearsay? Was he like the Pole of whom he had spoken, an unmitigated liar?

The bus drew up in front of a restaurant and the driver said, "Well, folks, this is where you get your refreshments." Trevor stayed where he was, not feeling like eating, while the others woke as from the dead, rubbing their eyes, stretching.

"You wouldn't recognize your brother now," he heard Douglas saying. And then he heard his brother's voice, "You didn't even do your National Service."

Three

HE ARRIVED IN Sydney at ten o'clock at night and wasn't
prepared for the size of the city. Why, it was at least as big as
London and probably bigger, with tall buildings thrusting
aggressively into the sky, a jungle of lights. In relation to
Canberra it had a powerful, pushy air. From the bus station
he took a taxi, giving the name of the hotel, which at first the
driver couldn't find. They drove around a park while the
driver kept saying,

"I can't see it, mate. Are you sure it's on Elizabeth
Street." For a moment Trevor was terrified he had made a
mistake till he checked the address in his book.

"I was definitely told Elizabeth Street," he said, and
eventually after they had driven two or three times round the
park he was the first to see the name, the Australia Hotel,
among the other competing signs on the street. It surprised
him that the entrance was so small and insignificant, since the
name itself sounded so grand.

When he eventually pressed the bell he heard a dis-
embodied voice speaking to him, asking him to identify
himself, for the door was locked. After he had said who he

was the door opened slowly, creaking gently as it did so, and, as he entered, it shut behind him. What on earth was this? He felt as if he was entering a dilapidated prison. The building was like a slum in Glasgow.

"Sixth floor," the voice had said.

By main force he pushed open the door of an ancient lift and pressed the button for the sixth floor, rising as if he were inside an old metallic coffin. How did this place have the nerve to call itself the Australian Hotel: why, it was like a grimy midnight tomb. The lift door opened and he found himself at what appeared to be a reception desk behind which sat a young, dark-skinned man with a moustache.

"The tab from the Tourist Bureau?" the man said, and Trevor handed the tab over, all the time looking uneasily about him. Planks of wood were leaning against the ancient wall: it was as though he had interrupted workmen in shoring up the building. He felt tense and frightened.

"We like our guests to pay in advance," said the dark-skinned man. "How long are you staying for?"

"A week," said Trevor, not knowing until then what answer he would give. He felt extremely tired after his long journey and nearly fled down the stairs. Why should he be asked to pay a week in advance for such a grimy place? But at the same time he was afraid that if he changed his mind he would be able to find no accommodation elsewhere at such a late hour. He took the required money out of his wallet and handed it over.

"Will you be wanting breakfast?" said the man.

"Yes," said Trevor, "half-past eight if that is convenient." His voice sounded strange to himself, almost echoing and nervous.

The man made a note on the pad in front of him and

Trevor re-entered the lift. It was while he was travelling funereally down to the floor on which his room was that he suddenly realized that he hadn't been given a receipt for his money. But he didn't feel able to return and ask for one. There was something overwhelmingly seedy about the hotel, something almost derelict and evil. He felt that it was a place where transients and vagrants stayed and in his fevered imagination it became a den where knife fights were common, where screams were heard from the desperate and the weak, where there were sudden explosions of violence. A vision of the college rose up in front of him with nostalgic intensity, and he saw a man sweeping leaves from the lawn and dumping them into a wheelbarrow. The man moved with rustic, timeless slowness.

He wished that there was someone whom he could talk to, confide in, some third person who would be able to confer reality on the flickering world in which he now seemed to be living, some disinterested judge who would be sane and ordinary and clear-thinking. As he scurried along the flaking corridor to his room, he noticed scars on doors, and once he had a glimpse of a huge negro in shirt sleeves coming out of a bathroom. When he had opened the door of his room with the key he had been provided with, he immediately locked it behind him, shivering uncontrollably. Sweating profusely he sat down on the only chair in the room, leaving his small case on the floor beside him.

He looked around him. There was a cracked basin fitted into the wall, but when he ran the water it made a thunderous stuttering noise as he washed his face which was streaming with perspiration. The walls and ceiling were spotted with brown stains as if there was some disease haunting the room, some sordid plague. As he sat down he heard a high, piercing whine like that of a mosquito. He went to the window to peer out but it was covered with wire netting, though it was partially open. Across from him he could see a dark building which looked like a factory.

He felt suddenly in desperate need of a pee but at the same time was frightened lest he might be waylaid in the corridor, for he felt himself, in his feverish fear, surrounded by secret, violent people. Throughout the whole hotel there was an ominous, palpitating silence. Eventually he couldn't contain himself any longer, opened the door carefully and seeing no one crept into the adjacent bathroom where there was a dirty shower and a toilet around which there were old, damp, dirty papers.

After peeing he returned quickly to his room and locked the door again. He was angry that he had found himself in such a place, angry that he had paid in advance. He sat down on the bed and considered. Now that he had paid in advance he would have to wait there for a week. On the other hand might it not be better to sacrifice the money he had already paid and find a better hotel? Still, he wasn't rich and if he found his brother destitute he would need all the money he had in order to help him. He should have phoned Sheila, that's what he should have done, but some instinct made him decide against doing so. He had half expected that there might have been a phone in his hotel room but there wasn't. And he didn't want to speak to that dark-skinned man again, climb to the sixth floor in that creaking hearse-like lift, and ask him where he could phone from.

Now for the morning. He would have to find the Births, Marriages and Deaths office, and discover if his brother's name was on the list of those who had died. How far back did their records go? And what if his brother had given a wrong name to the police as Douglas had suggested he might have done? What if the police had covered up his death, if he had in fact died in a cell? Were the police in Sydney as violent as they appeared to be in other countries? He tried to think if he had read anything about them in newspapers or magazines but couldn't remember any references to them.

Slightly dizzy with tiredness and tension he heard the liquid burble of a police car followed by the whine of an ambulance racing through the night and was aware of the weight and randomness and resonance of the city around him, busy and impersonal, with its cargoes of separate people. What if something happened to him here? He hadn't told anyone where he was staying, and if anything happened he didn't think that anyone would be intelligent enough to contact the Tourist Bureau. He cursed himself for being so stupid as not to have left an address behind him in Canberra. He had had a whole day to make his preparations and he had omitted a precaution as obvious as that. The room oppressed him and the whine of the mosquito, if that was what it was, was getting on his nerves. What were these marks on the walls, brown, almost obscene, a strange astronomy of dirty stars? He shivered, thinking that this might be the sort of place his brother would be used to. No, much worse than this.

He undressed slowly and got between the sheets which seemed to be clean enough. But then would one be able to see fleas with the naked eye?

He wished that he had a drink but then thought of his brother and decided that he didn't want one. He took a book from his case and tried to read it but couldn't concentrate. Then he took out a magazine and tried to read that. It was called *The Bulletin* and there was an article in it about oil drilling, and whether it should be permitted along the Barrier Reef. He glanced through the story without much interest.

What in fact would he discover in the morning? Would he find that his brother was indeed dead? Please God let that not happen, he prayed. He had a vision of his brother dead in a foreign land, buried in a desert across which the wind and sand swirled continually. He saw him in a nameless grave, unilluminated, drab. He looked down at himself as he lay in the bed, white and shrouded. And then he thought of Sheila again. That had been the worst: but what could they have done about it? Nothing. It had happened, and that was all that could be said about it. And it had been the reason why his brother had gone to Australia. At the time both he and Sheila had decided that it had been the fortunes of war, but how had Norman felt about it all?

As he lay there staring up at the spotted ceiling, scenes from the past unwound in front of his eyes. His brother, at the wedding, generous as always with drink, was growing more and more obstreperous. He himself was trying to calm him down, thinking at the same time how uncultured he was, how boorish, how exhibitionist and extravagant. He had the strange sensation that his brother had actually been in the very hotel he himself was now in, that he had slept in the same bed, that at that very moment he was watching him and smiling like that fellow Douglas.

As there was no bedside lamp he had to get up to put out the light at the wall switch and then creep back across the bare room in his bare feet. He lay in the darkness thinking, and after a while slept.

Four

IN THE MORNING as the sun streamed in through the wire-netted window the room suddenly seemed less threatening, more ordinary. Even the furniture — such as it was — didn't appear so scarred, and the whining of the mosquito, if such it had been, had ceased. But when he looked down at his arms he saw that they were covered with big red weals. My God, he thought, how did this happen? It must have been fleas or mosquitoes. He must find a chemist and buy some sort of antidote. He felt suddenly dirty in spite of the bright new sunlight around him. When there was a knock at the door and a man wheeled his breakfast in he almost mentioned the fleas or mosquitoes in his frustration and fury, but then prudently decided against doing so.

After eating his cornflakes and toast, and drinking his tea, he resolved to go out immediately. Locking the door carefully behind him — after he had wheeled the tray with the breakfast things out of the room — he descended by the stairs rather than enter the old rickety lift which had seemed so much like a cage or a coffin. He opened the main door on to the dazzle of a fine warm morning. As he walked down

Elizabeth Street by the side of the park he was caught up in the rush of people hurrying to their work, many of them in shirt sleeves and shorts, looking relaxed yet purposeful. It was as if he had become part of a natural moving world again.

He made his way in the direction of the harbour for he had found out from his map of the city where the offices of Births, Marriages and Deaths were. Ahead of him he saw tall, powerful buildings and was gripped by a sense of their dizzying solidity. Why, there must be at least 60 floors in some of these offices. He glanced to his right into the park and seeing a bald man lying face down on the grass, a bottle beside him, suddenly shivered. His own brother might be like that, abandoned, derelict, helpless. The only consolation was that the weather never seemed to be cold, not even in the autumn, and there was hardly ever any rain. His brother would have been worse off in Glasgow.

His arms itched and the red weals looked angry and swollen and he stopped at a chemist's shop and asked the man behind the counter if he could do something about them.

"Fleas, sir, that's what they are," said the chemist. Trevor almost told him about the hotel but decided not to in case there might be trouble which he couldn't afford to become involved in. After he had left the chemist's he put the ointment, which he had been given, on his spots, feeling dirty and soiled as he saw the tall, long-legged, tanned men and women striding past him to their work.

At last he arrived at the building he was seeking and saw that the office he required was on the eighth floor. He entered a lift with a lot of chattering girls who seemed to be clerkesses and typists. The lift flickered with lights like a huge computer and he finally emerged on to the correct floor. A sign said NO SMOKING but he saw as he went into the office that three girls were standing beside a desk smoking and talking in animated tones, while casually examining their nails.

"I have an inquiry to make," he said to a young girl who was sitting in front of a typewriter. "I want to know whether a relative of mine, a brother in fact, is dead. I was told recently that he had died. I am only in Australia for a short while."

She gazed at him unsmilingly and he almost shouted, "Can't you see that it is my brother I am talking about." It seemed to him that the whole world should share his own sorrow.

"If you wait here for a moment I'll see about it," said the girl, and left him. As he waited he saw people standing at ledges filling in forms of different colours, some pink, some blue. He imagined that some of the documents might be in connection with births rather than deaths, blue for boys and pink for girls, and again he was desolated with sorrow. Perhaps he was the only person there inquiring about a death.

The girl came back and indicated a man who was standing behind a desk.

"I would like you to fill in a form," said the man. "We want to know why you are investigating the death of your brother."

"I was told . . ." Trevor began.

"I know," said the man, who appeared to Trevor to be remote and unsympathetic. "But we have a policy of not releasing information to just anyone. I hope you can understand why that should be. You're not Australian? You're here on holiday?"

"No," said Trevor, "I'm not Australian. I'm Scottish."

"Well," said the man, "I know that in Britain you

impose fewer checks. But you can easily see that problems are involved. For example you could be looking for your brother for financial gain. That's why we wish you to fill in this form. We'll let you know in a few days.''

"In a few days,'' said Trevor in an agitated manner. "I thought you would let me know today. I'm only in Sydney till tomorrow morning,'' he lied. "I'm here from Canberra and I've got to go back tomorrow morning. I am working in a college there.''

"We'll see what we can do then,'' said the man, "if you fill in the form.'' He's taken a dislike to me, thought Trevor, he won't come back, he won't bother looking for the information. In any case what evidence have I that Norman was ever in Sydney, was ever in a police station? He filled in the form which asked him about his relationship with the presumed deceased. I am his brother, thought Trevor, I am searching for him simply because he is my brother, I do not expect financial gain, I have no ulterior motive. How could I profit from him if he has no money? And he was suddenly convinced that Norman was dead. As he handed the man the form his heart was beating furiously and he had broken out in a sweat. This man, he thought, looks so callous, he doesn't realize what this means to me, he has never been in the same situation, how can he possibly understand? I should have sent Norman money, he thought, I should have tried to find him. But I was too occupied with my own selfish interests. And now perhaps this man guesses all this. He felt naked and ashamed in the office in which the three girls were still talking.

"So we went to this restaurant,'' one of them was saying,'' and we had this marvellous fish, bream I think it was.'' The others looked at her with polite disinterest. The rest of the world continues its existence, thought Trevor, it's only I who am standing here in a daze of sorrow waiting for that bureaucrat to examine his macabre records. He saw a woman happily filling in a pink form. Who would have known when Norman was born that he would end up in Australia? One of the girls poured out smoke from a discontented mouth.

Suddenly the man was there in front of him. How had he so quickly searched the records? They must have a computer, that was the only possibility. He had a paper in his hand and at that moment Trevor knew with desolate certainty that his brother was indeed dead and that this bureaucrat whom he had never met in his life till now was about to tell him the most dreadful news. It must be Norman's death certificate that he was holding in his hands. But even while Trevor stood there in a daze the man was saying,

"We have no record at all of your brother's death."

"What? What?" said Trevor in amazement and confusion.

"I said there is no record."

Suddenly Trevor began to babble almost hysterically, "Are you sure? Is there any possibility that he could have been buried under another name? Someone said," and he brought the words out with difficulty, "that he had died in a police cell."

"There is no chance of that at all," said the man, whom Trevor could now see was humane and compassionate, and indeed glad that his brother was not dead. "None at all. He would have been identified by someone. He would have been traced. If he had a record they would have his fingerprints. No, he is not dead. He certainly didn't die here."

Trevor felt like shouting with joy and embracing the man: the world was beautifully managed after all, the bureaucrats

39

had their place in it, they toiled among the records, it was necessary for them to be dispassionate like surgeons, accurate and conscientious. They could be like angels bearing good news.

The man was holding out the paper towards him. "That is your certificate stating that as far as our records show he isn't dead." And he named a fee which Trevor hardly heard as he pulled out his wallet. He would have given the man all the money he had.

More carefree than he had felt for a long time he put the certificate in his wallet and left the office, to be replaced by a fat man who was making an inquiry of his own. But as he was descending the stairs he knew that he couldn't leave it at that. His brother was apparently not dead — that he must now accept — but his responsibility did not end there. He might be living in poverty and destitution. He felt himself as a white knight sent by an irrevocable and mysterious destiny to save him. Surely he must have been sent to Australia for that very reason, surely there was a profound, enigmatic fate that had directed him on this mission. He climbed the stairs and went back.

"Is there a Missing Persons Bureau at the Police Station?" he asked. The man gave him an address and Trevor thanked him. This time he decided to take the lift and descended smoothly in the large box with its flashing lights to the ground floor.

He took a taxi to the Missing Persons Bureau and was more talkative than he usually was.

"This is a big city you have here," he said to the taxi driver.

"It's big enough. I was born and bred here and there's still parts of it I don't know."

"It seems bigger than London," said Trevor. "And yet the people look more relaxed."

"You Scotch?" said the taxi driver.

"That's right. I'm here from Canberra."

"Canberra, eh?"

"Do you like living in Sydney?" Trevor enquired.

"Greatest city in the world. I've never been out of it."

When the taxi drew up at the police station Trevor gave the driver a tip though he knew that tips were not expected nor looked for.

"That's your place there," said the taxi driver. "Have a good day."

Certainly so far it had been a good day, thought Trevor, for he had at least discovered that his brother was alive. Nevertheless he might find out bad news at the Bureau. Was it after all the case that, as Douglas had said, his brother had a police record? Had he been in a cell? Had he been a thief?

Told by a guard on the ground floor that the office was higher up, he took a lift and got out. He knocked on the door of the office and found a detective there.

He told him his story and the detective listened politely and attentively, now and again asking a question. He seems friendly enough, thought Trevor, he doesn't look like the sort of person who might beat a drunk or thief to death. But how did one recognize that kind of person? After all in a big city where policemen confronted violent criminals they themselves were likely to become violent in self-defence.

"How long since you actually heard from him?" said the detective who was a big man in shirt sleeves.

"About eighteen years ago," said Trevor. "I realize that is a long time ago but I was neglectful and I had much else to do. I didn't keep in touch. I should have tried to write but

41

latterly I didn't have an address to write to."

The detective gazed at him without comment. "I suppose it's because he's in his shirt sleeves," Trevor thought, "that he looks so harmless and relaxed."

At the same time it occurred to him that for a job of this kind they would pick a friendly, affable person.

"Can you tell me what he looks like? Height, details like that," said the detective, drawing a note pad towards him.

Trevor hesitated for a moment. What had his brother looked like? Had his eyes been blue? Yes, blue, surely they had been blue. Distinguishing marks? Had there been any? He couldn't remember any. He gave his brother's height as five feet eight, though he wasn't sure. He added lightly, "He may be going bald now. There's baldness in the family."

The detective didn't smile but asked him for his brother's date of birth.

"He's two years younger than me," said Trevor. "That will make him thirty-nine." Thirty-nine? Was his brother really thirty-nine? He thought of him as an eternal twenty. Somehow he couldn't imagine Norman as thirty-nine.

Date of birth?

It was sometime in April surely. But Trevor couldn't remember the exact day. Had there been some joke about Shakespeare? Had he been born on the same day as Shakespeare had been?

"No," he said at last. "I can't remember. It was some time in April."

"But then," he added, "he might not have given his real name."

"Why not?" said the detective.

"Well, to be perfectly honest," said Trevor in a burst of

candour, "I heard that he might have died in the cells here."

"Go on."

"That's what I was told. A man got in touch with me in Canberra. He said that a Pole had told him that my brother had died in the cells here. He said that the Pole had been at one time in the same lodgings as my brother. The Pole's name was . . ." Forgetting the name Trevor took out his address book in which he had copied it down.

"Sikowski, that was the Pole's name according to my informant."

"I see," said the detective equably. "When was this supposed to have happened?"

"You mean, when was I told?"

"No, when was he supposed to have died in the cells?"

"Recently," said Trevor. "But my informant told me that this Pole might have been lying, for some reason of his own."

Was he imagining it or had the detective become more watchful after hearing his last statements?

"And how did this man get in touch with you?"

"I was giving a talk on the radio," said Trevor. "He heard my name and my accent and he thought I might be related to this Norman Grierson whom he had known."

"He phoned you?"

"That's right."

The detective pondered for a moment and then said,

"You had never heard of this man before?"

"No, never."

And then it occurred to him that this man Douglas might not have given his correct name either. If his brother could change his name, why couldn't he? Perhaps if he rang the number he had been given there would be no answer. He remembered that Douglas had hesitated a little when he had been asked for his phone number. He himself should have verified the existence of the number before leaving Canberra but there were so many things he had done wrong, or had neglected doing. It had been very foolish of him not to have attempted some confirmation.

"It sounds strange," said the detective at last.

"But there was another thing," said Trevor. "He told me that my brother had been in trouble with the law." For some reason he heard himself adding, "I find this very odd, too. I am over here from Scotland and lecturing in Canberra University."

"I see," said the detective making another note. Trevor felt calmer. It was as if now that he had placed his brother's fate in the hands of these official people he might in some way be relieved of responsibility.

The detective picked up the phone with his left hand, cradling it against his cheek while doodling on the note pad in front of him with his right hand.

"A Norman Grierson," he said. "Do we have anything on him." He gave the details he had received from Trevor and after a while put the phone down. He gazed mildly at Trevor and said,

"They'll ring back."

Suddenly Trevor said, "He might be an alcoholic. Do many alcoholics go missing like this?"

"Some," said the detective, and Trevor got the impression that he had asked a stupid question. As the two of them sat in silence like conspirators he imagined a computer racing through name after name in some room far from where he was waiting.

44

Eventually the phone broke the almost sleepy silence and the detective listened, beginning to doodle again.

"Uh huh. When was that? I see. Nothing else? Right."

He put the phone down and said, "Yes, we do have something on him. Nothing big. He was arrested once for being drunk and disorderly. That was back in 'sixty-five."

"What would have happened to him?" said Trevor urgently.

"He would have been fined. It was a minor offence. Do you know if he's been working?"

"My informant seemed to think he had been working at times."

"Well, I'm afraid that's all we have," said the detective.

"What about other states?" said Trevor. "What if he has moved and is no longer in Sydney."

The detective looked at him in the same calm considering manner and picked up the phone again.

"About Grierson," he said. "Anything on him in the other states?" Trevor imagined his brother lying drunk in some corner of Sydney even while he himself was talking to this tranquil, relaxed detective, and, panic stricken, felt that every moment was crucial. Even computers might not be fast enough to save him.

The phone rang again and his stomach tightened.

"Uh huh," said the detective. "Nothing?" He doodled. Trevor tried to see what the casual scrawls meant, as if they might tell him the secret, unconscious thoughts of the detective, but couldn't make any sense of them.

"I see," said the detective and put the phone down.

He looked at Trevor and said, "Nothing. He doesn't appear in any other records."

If that is the only entry they have on him, thought

Trevor, it might mean he's dead after all. And again he was overwhelmed by a mounting wave of sorrow.

"I'm sorry," said the detective, "that is all I can do at the moment. But of course we can continue our enquiries. Do you want us to do that?"

"Yes, please," said Trevor. "I would like that. If you would be so kind." He gave the detective his phone number and address in Canberra and then stood up.

"Thank you," he said. "Thank you for all your trouble." But as he was thanking the detective he thought of himself as a traitor to his brother. Maybe Norman had been in fact beaten up in the cells and the police were concealing his dim, sordid death. To them, after all, he might have been just another drifter: how could they possibly see him as Trevor saw him? Maybe he had been dumped into a vagrant's grave with no flowers and no headstone.

And yet, like a servile peasant, he said, "Thank you" a third time. Had he not grown up in a society where good manners, even hypocrisy, were the rule? Was the society where people beat each other up and fought and starved the real one?

"If anything turns up I shall be in touch," said the detective mildly. Trevor walked to the lift and took it to the ground floor, feeling desolated once more. His destiny seemed to be to rise and descend in lifts, anonymous, remote, enclosed. He despised himself for not remembering his brother's birthday and for not remembering him as clearly as he should have done. How could he exist in the world if he had no memory or observation? And yet he could remember quite clearly the date of birth of Robert Louis Stevenson, the date on which *Kidnapped* had been published, and for that matter the date of *The Master of*

46

Ballantrae, that story about two brothers, one of whom had hated the other. Nevertheless he couldn't remember the colour of his own brother's eyes.

As he made his way along the street, among all the others embroiled in the concerns of the day, he felt detached from the world around him as if he were in free fall.

What am I going to do next, he thought. Haven't I done enough? Is more expected of me? And he felt obscurely that he couldn't leave things as they were. It was as if the riddle of his brother's life and presumed death reared up in the forefront of his consciousness, demanding a solution: it was like seeing a question in the shape of a snake.

There must be some other place he could try. What did people do when they couldn't find relatives, had lost touch with them? Considering the problem he went into a café and ordered coffee. How clean and hygienic all the public places in Australia were. Napkins: beautiful coffee with lovely rich cream. But he didn't feel at all hungry and the euphoria of discovering that his brother wasn't dead had worn off. How huge and incalculable this city was. His brother could be anywhere in it, or he might be in some other town or city in some other state. Or perhaps he had never been in Sydney at all. Well, yes, he had, he had been, for there was that arrest for being drunk and disorderly. He wondered why his brother had come to the city at all. Might he not have been better off in the country?

On an impulse he rushed outside and found a public phone box and rang the number which Douglas had given him. The phone rang and rang but there was no answer. Had Douglas given him a wrong number? Or was he at work? But he had said that he was working on a book and if that was the case he should be at home.

As he came out of the phone box he saw an aborigine crossing the street against the DON'T WALK sign, swaying drunkenly. The aborigine was muttering to himself and glaring at the passers by. If it weren't for the colour, that could be my brother, thought Trevor. He too could be staggering along and cursing the universe. And again he had the feeling that his brother was in grave danger and only a quick intervention would save him.

The monotonous sun shone down on him and he felt sweaty again, his white shirt sticking to him, his arms itchy. He shouldn't have worn his jacket. He should have left it in his room but if he had done that he would have had no pocket in which to carry his wallet. And again if he had left it behind someone might have stolen it. He wondered as he walked along the street if the Australians recognized him for the foreigner he was, as he himself for instance could easily identify Americans in Glasgow with their white hats and white suits and cigars. There might even be a trembling uncertainty about the way in which he carried himself. In the whole city he didn't know a single soul.

And then as he was thinking this, he realized where he might go. The Salvation Army of course. He went up to two policemen who were at that very moment crossing the road and asked them where the Salvation Army offices were. One looked at the other and scratched his head, and finally both admitted that they didn't know.

At that very moment, by an enormous coincidence, Trevor saw the Salvation Army offices opposite him. He was back on Elizabeth Street and not far away from his hotel.

Five

As HE WALKED to the Salvation Army office his mind
gnawed at what the detective in the Missing Persons Bureau
had told him. He had said that his brother had not been in
trouble with the police in Sydney apart from the minor
offence of drunkenness. In that case why had Douglas given
him the impression that he had been an habitual criminal? He
had for instance mentioned something about a brick, and
breaking and entering. Either the police were lying or
Douglas was lying. What did he in fact know about
Douglas? Nothing much except that he was married and had
a child - or so he thought he had said. He had also said that he
had been in trouble with the police himself. But if he had a
wife and child and was also, as he said, working on a book,
why was there no answer from his phone? Surely there ought
to be someone in the house, if not Douglas himself, then
perhaps his wife. Perhaps he had given a wrong number and a
wrong name. There was something odd about him, signified
by his secret laughter, almost as if he was involved in a deep,
enigmatic plot against Trevor, who had the distinct impression that Douglas hated him and people like him. Perhaps he

despised teachers and lecturers and those whom he considered lived in an unreal world. He had certainly acted as if he despised Trevor's mentality. When listening to the local radio Trevor had detected a strong streak of radicalism, for many of the programmes were about the oppressed among whom were numbered women, the unemployed, the Irish. In ideology Douglas seemed to be on the same wavelength, except that there was a wayward, unpredictable vein of violence which Trevor sensed in him. Was Australia as classless a society as he had been told or were there strata of social differences even here? No, he felt that, though perhaps not as clearly defined as elsewhere, classes were fixed and present in this large, astonishing country.

Trevor remembered the taxi driver he had once driven with in Canberra when he was returning to the college late at night after seeing a play by Brecht. The man had told him that that very evening he had taken a woman and her child to a house of a friend of hers. It was in one of the poor areas of the city, the driver had told him, and the woman had said, on arriving at her destination, that she had no money but that she would borrow her fare from her friend. All the time she had been in the taxi the driver had been suspicious of her, for there had exuded from her a dreadful smell, as if of drugs, and the face of the child was covered in blotches and spots. After a while she had come back from the house saying that there was no one at home and confessing that she had no money. And then she had said, "I'll give you my ring. You keep it and when I have money I'll collect it."

"I still have the ring in the office," the taxi driver had told Trevor, "But she never came for it." As he was being told the story Trevor saw sheet lightning illuminating the city and heard rumblings of thunder.

"But what could I do?" said the taxi driver who was a large, calm man, "I have to earn my living." At that time Trevor had thought little of the story but now it came back to him with guilt and fear: in a small anonymous office he saw a ring lying on a table. He also remembered the polite, studious audience which had listened attentively to Brecht's attack on the rich, the ironic paradoxical bleakness of the dialogue. He recognized some of the lecturers from the college among the audience but he didn't go and speak to them, though they had always been kind to him. Those who could afford the high price of the tickets were watching a play which wasn't addressed to them at all, but rather to those who couldn't pay, the oppressed, the unbeautiful, the unemployed.

On the contrary the beautiful and the rich with their brandy glasses made a golden circle of brilliance in his mind. Everywhere in the world there were the powerful ones who stood around in a ring drinking brandy and on the outside of this secret masonry were the unfortunate and the poor and the destitute. He wondered what was happening to him since he had arrived in Australia. Was he developing a social conscience? Curiously, in Glasgow, an infinitely more deprived city than any he had seen here, a social conscience hadn't troubled him. Did he have to come to a new place to see the distorted figures of the poor and the handicapped?

"Bobby Burns," that other driver had said to him on learning that he was Scottish. "You come from the land of Bobby Burns, eh? There's a statue to him here. Bobby Burns, he was a great one for the sheilas, wasn't he?"

His brother's friends had not been his friends. Sometimes Norman brought them home and he couldn't find anything to say to them. All they seemed to be interested in was

51

women and drink. But then there had been Sheila as well. Maybe he shouldn't have done that but he couldn't help himself: and now what was happening to his marriage? Had she not belonged to his brother's set as well? Had she not worked in the same factory as him? He had never even visited the factory and yet his brother had come to have a look at his own room in the university.

"I couldn't work here," he had said. "I couldn't work in a place like this. Too quiet."

Trevor stopped in front of the Salvation Army office.

Six

THE LADY IN charge of the Missing Persons Bureau of the
Salvation Army was called Mrs Tennant. She was plump,
matronly, and efficient. In front of her on the desk Trevor
noticed a bottle of pills.

"I'm just back at work after an illness," she said. "Well,
then," she went on, her voice becoming more brisk, "you're
looking for your brother. And you say he's not dead." She
studied the document that he had been given at the office of
Births, Marriages and Deaths.

"According to this man — what was his name again . . .
Douglas — your brother was in Sydney and as far as he knows
may still be there. I hope you realize what you are letting
yourself in for if you find him. You say you want him to come
home but he may not want to. Again he may be a confirmed
alcoholic. We had a lady from England who took her son
home, paid a great deal of money for his ticket, and shortly
afterwards he disappeared again. She doesn't know where he
is. That's the sort of thing you have to take account of. Do
you understand me? Now I've got some sources that I don't
normally divulge."

She spoke into the phone for a while. "This is a lady," she said, putting her hand over the mouthpiece, "who does a lot of good work for me. If he's in Sydney she should know about it."

She put the phone down.

"She should ring back in ten minutes or so. Of course there's Social Security if he's not working. There's the voting roll but if what you tell me is true he might not have registered, though voting is compulsory in Australia as you will no doubt know. When did you last see him?"

"When he left for Australia," Trevor replied.

"And that was nearly twenty years ago, as far as I can gather."

"Eighteen."

"The other thing is that he might have left Sydney. A lot of them go to Queensland."

"Queensland?"

"Yes." She didn't elaborate why she thought he might have moved to Queensland.

"If he's working he's all right," said Mrs Tennant. "Did he have a trade when he came out? What did he use to do?"

"He didn't have a trade. He was working in a factory. He used to make clocks."

"I would imagine he would be depending on casual labour then. There's a high rate of unemployment in Australia at the moment. That's what a lot of people in Britain don't understand. They still think of Australia as a colony whose streets are paved with gold. Did you know there was a good deal of unemployment?"

"I saw some slogans students had written on walls in Canberra. And I've read the papers. I've gathered there's unemployment."

"You say this fellow Douglas got out of the 'system', as he called it. Your brother might have been fortunate enough to do the same: he might have come to his senses, broken the habit of drink. He might even have gone to another city to escape an environment that was harming him. Had you thought of that?"

"I understood there's a high rate of unemployment all over Australia," said Trevor.

"There is." And then she added inconsequentially. "I'm just back from England myself. I belong originally to Surrey. I go home every three years or so."

Trevor nearly made a remark about Mrs Thatcher but decided against it: for all he knew Mrs Tennant might be a Tory of unclouded blue though that was hardly likely. It occurred to him that, matronly as she appeared, she must be quite tough, and had certainly seen far more of life than he had.

The telephone rang and she picked it up. She listened carefully, now and again scribbling on a writing pad. When she had finished speaking she said to Trevor:

"She can't find any trace of him, and he does not seem to be in the Social Security records which might mean one of two things, either that he's moved to some other state or that he's working."

Or, thought Trevor, that he's dead.

"You don't think there's any possibility he might be dead," he said tentatively.

"Well, you do have that document which suggests that he isn't. All you can do is leave the case with us and we'll see if we can come up with anything. I would have thought there would have been some trace somewhere. Some of them come to us if they're derelict. You say that he's been in trouble with the police?"

55

"I was told that he had been once but only for a minor offence."

"They usually tend to continue in that way which is why it surprises me that no one has heard of him since. However he may have managed to leave Sydney as your friend Douglas did. It would have been better for him to do so."

"Is it a violent city?" asked Trevor, thinking of the police, the cell, the Pole.

"Not specially. It's a big city and there's naturally some violence. I wouldn't say the murder rate was high. But of course as in any big city you will find deprivation. Not everybody is affluent. It wouldn't compare with some other big cities for violence."

She stood up and held her hand out. "Don't worry. If he can be found we will find him and after that we will see what can be done. I would advise you, when we do, not to give him any large sum of money. He would only drink it if what I suspect is true. Do you understand?"

"Yes, I understand."

"In that case, go and God bless you. We will pray for him and hope for the best. Was he at all religious?"

"I don't think so. He didn't go to church."

"I was afraid of that. Sometimes their early training helps in difficult situations."

"Thank you at any rate for what you have done," said Trevor. This woman was from choice immersing herself in the dark element and yet she looked sunny and calm and radiant as if deriving strength and light from the darkness into which she peered. He thought of all the forces in the world that were bent on alleviating the harm that might come to the strugglers in life, the irretrievably wounded ones, the headlong, careless youthful ones. With their trumpets and bugles and cornets and drums he imagined the Salvation Army marching into the slums, sustained by faith, eternally triumphant, an army of soldiers with ragged flags.

"Thank you again," he said, and left the office. As he was descending the stairs he didn't know what he would do next, or where he should go. He thought that perhaps now he had done enough. Should he not leave it at that and return to Canberra where he felt at home? He had an intense desire akin to thirst on a hot day to go to a library and sit there and read book after book for hours. The desire was so strong that it felt like an addiction. On the other hand what a triumph it would be if he could find his brother and take him home with him from the terrors and darknesses of the big anonymous city. But he didn't know where to start and then as he stood once again on the street it occurred to him that he did know where to start. Douglas had mentioned some lodging house where derelicts stayed. What was it called again? He took out his address book, and studied it in the warm, bright sunlight. The Michael Tarrant Home. Why shouldn't he go there? Could he not find him there perhaps or if not him the Pole who had started him off on his odyssey? At the same time he was afraid of descending into those depths and for a moment felt dizzy. He was certainly an innocent abroad himself. Still, if he went back to Canberra now he would forever after wonder where his brother was and regret that he had not done more to find him. He almost heard his phantom voice in the dazzle of the day.

Without his knowing it he arrived opposite a bookshop which sold Greek books. He studied them through the window, but couldn't understand what the titles meant. This was all Greek to him, he considered wryly. In any case it was modern Greek, not the ancient Greek of Homer, not the

57

musical phrases of Ulysses and the other heroes.

He took out his map and studied it. Yes, Douglas had given him the area the Home was in: it was near the docks. He began to walk towards them. If he had been on holiday in Sydney he would have gone to visit the Opera House which he had studied on a postcard once, scallop on scallop of it, a huge shell which would at times resonate with music. Perhaps he might even have sailed round the famous harbour. But he didn't have the leisure or the inclination to do that in his present state of mind, and he felt sorry for himself with his spotty, inflamed arms, and his confused feelings. He kept on walking, his feet sore from the stone of the pavements. Perhaps he should eat? But he didn't feel like eating. To eat was to remember his brother and others like him, and to imagine their hunger. The red lights glared continually ahead of him. DON'T WALK, they said, DON'T WALK.

It was like wandering through a waste land. Fragments of Eliot's poem returned to him, the incurable detritus of academe. "Phlebas the Phoenician drowned . . ." Curious how even now his literary training haunted him.

It took him some time to find the Home and then only after he had asked a number of people who looked at him in a suspicious manner. What was a well-dressed man like him doing searching for such a place? When he found it he rang the bell and a big man in shirt sleeves came to the door.

"I'm looking for someone, my brother in fact," said Trevor. The man looked at him and said,

"What is his name?"

Trevor told him and the man said, "We get so many people moving through here. Transients. Come in. I have a book here but I can't recall such a name. Mine by the way is Mason. Mark Mason."

"Trevor Grierson."

"Well, Trevor, you know how it is here. We give them a bed and food." He scratched his shiny bald head and said, "I can't remember that name. But maybe . . ."

He led Trevor into a room which looked like a barracks, or what he imagined a barracks might be like, and in which there was a number of beds, on one of which a man with a bearded, pale, gaunt face was sitting. His little eyes like those of a cornered rat darted at first from side to side and then finally fixed on Trevor steadily.

"This is Henry," said Mason. "Henry Morton. Isn't that right, Henry? Henry's been here for some time."

The small beady eyes turned from Mason to Trevor and seemed to be examining the latter closely. Trevor felt his skin begin to crawl and thought, "My brother might be like this now." The pointed bluish nose was a signal of decay and alcoholism. It darted from side to side like a needle on a speedometer.

"I'll leave you with Henry," said Mason, "I have a few things to do." He looked large and harassed as if aware that only by luck had he himself avoided the condition of the inmates of his Home.

"There's a bell at the desk if you want to contact me. If anyone knows anything about your brother Henry here will know, won't you, Henry? He spoke as if he had been learning from a book how inmates were to be spoken to and treated. Henry stared at him blankly.

Trevor sat down on the edge of the bed which he felt must be a pullulating arena of fleas and lice. The walls looked old and discoloured and it seemed to Trevor they hadn't been painted for years. He felt for a moment dizzy and disoriented.

"I'm looking," he began carefully, "for a brother of mine.

59

His name is Norman, Norman Grierson. Has he been here at all?''

Henry was staring at him with quick, intelligent eyes, trying to document his clothes, his appearance, his air of prosperity, and perhaps his foreign innocence.

"Norman Grierson," he mumbled, "Norman Grierson."

"Yes, that's his name," said Trevor impatiently.

Henry glanced down at Trevor's shoes and then at his face again. His Adam's apple moved like a squirrel that is rapidly ascending and descending a wrinkled tree. Trevor noticed that the area round his sockets was pink like the feet of a dove he had once seen in a park in Glasgow. There too the unshaven men sat on benches all day, or haunted the reading rooms in their long coats that trailed to the ground. They wore scarves even in summer.

"I have a mate," said Henry at last. "He stays in a house near the docks. He knows your brother."

"What?" said Trevor excitedly.

"I knew him," said Henry. "I knew him myself. He spoke like you. He had the same voice."

"Like me?" said Trevor eagerly. "Go on."

"Yes, he used to work in Sydney. But I don't think he works now." And again he glanced at Trevor like a bright-eyed bird. Then he leaned forward, and Trevor felt the stench from him.

"He didn't work. The cops were after him."

"When? Where?" said Trevor.

"I can't remember," said Henry. "He moved out of here a long time ago and went and stayed with this mate of mine. My mate has a house," he said proudly.

"Why don't you stay with him then?" said Trevor.

"He doesn't want me. I stayed with him before and he put me out."

Trevor sensed again the little intelligent eyes scurrying all over his body, and he shifted away till he was sitting precariously on the very edge of the bed.

"His name's Harrison," said Henry and he gave Trevor the address.

"Do you know the Rocks?" he said. "Near there he stays."

"Are you sure it's my brother you're talking about?" said Trevor, and Henry answered,

"Norman Grierson. That's what you said. We used to call him Norm."

"Is he well?" asked Trevor. "Does he drink?"

"He's well," said Henry with the same air of profound secrecy. "He's well."

"How long has he been here?"

"Years and years," said Henry vaguely. And then leaning forward so that Trevor was almost overwhelmed by the stale smell of drink that emanated from the rotten furnace of his mouth,

"Can you give me any money?" His voice assumed the singsong tone of a beggar's. "Any money, mate?"

"Do you know anything else about my brother?" Trevor asked brusquely.

"Your brother. No, I don't know anything else about him. He speaks like you."

Trevor took a handful of coins from his pocket and handed them over. He said "Cheerio" to Morton and faced him as he backed away. He put his hand in his breast pocket to check that he still had his wallet and when he had left the room rang the bell at the desk. Mason came down a dark stair and asked him if he had discovered anything.

"Yes," said Trevor, "thank you. He knew of my brother. He gave me an address."

"Is that right?" said Mason, who seemed pleased that Morton had been of use. His arms had much black hair on them and on one was a tattooed blue anchor.

"I'm glad," he said, and the words sounded genteel and strange.

"Anyway thank you again for all your trouble," said Trevor who suddenly became very businesslike. "I'd better go and visit that address."

"Henry of course is a man who will do anything for money," said Mason. "Did you give him any?"

"I'm afraid I did."

"You realize of course," said Mason seriously, "that he might not know him at all. Some of them try to make themselves important by pretending to have information that they don't actually have. A lot of them will say what you expect them to say. They feel that information is power and they will do anything to be the centre of attention. Even kill," he added in a low voice.

"Kill?"

"Yes. Kill. One of them killed a mate of his last month. This mate of his clicked his teeth once too often so he was hit on the head with a hammer. God knows where the hammer came from. I've seen a lot of violence. I used to be a policeman myself till I landed this job."

"I have to go there anyway," said Trevor. "I can't afford not to. By the way, have you heard of a Pole called Sikowski?"

"Sikowski. Can't say that I have. No, the name doesn't ring a bell."

"Thank you anyway," said Trevor and left, passing a phone box on his way to the door.

Seven

TILL THE TIME came for him to go to the house where his brother was supposed to be staying (for Morton had suggested five o'clock on the grounds that he thought Harrison wouldn't be home till then from his work) Trevor went into a second-hand bookshop where there was a large number of paperbacks, including crime stories. He studied these, trying to find one that he hadn't read, and as he walked along the shelves, watched by a man who rocked gently in a chair while he read the Racing Page of the *Australian* he tried to assemble in his mind the details he had discovered. In the first place he had been told by two separate people, Douglas and Morton, that his brother had been in Sydney. It seemed plausible to assume that he was still there, though on the other hand it was odd that the Salvation Army could find no trace of him. But he had also to remember that both his informants didn't seem the most trustworthy of people: in fact both might be lying for some mysterious reason of their own. It was all very strange and opaque, as opaque as the dusty window of the shop in which he was at that moment standing.

As he leafed through a book by Ellery Queen — one from

the great period which he had already read — it occurred to him that he was himself taking part in a mystery in a manner of speaking. He felt himself at the centre of a devious intrigue which he was not equipped to unravel. And this feeling of helpless perplexity was reinforced when he went into a restaurant for some food, only to find that sitting at the adjoining table was Mrs Tennant whom at first he didn't recognize. She was sitting with another lady, as ample as herself, both of them wearing expensive grey blouses and necklaces, and when the two had finished their meal and were leaving Mrs Tennant came over to him and said, clasping his hands in hers,

"Don't worry, don't worry, we're working on it." He was astounded that out of a city of three million inhabitants she was the one who was sitting at the table next to him, and his feeling of being in a web intensified. He began to think of Douglas again. Was he in fact playing some deep game of his own, unstable and mocking as he had appeared? Was it even possible that he and Morton knew each other? But he couldn't think why Douglas should be deliberately deceiving him. Hadn't he after all taken the trouble to phone him? Shouldn't he feel more grateful to him than he actually did? But he felt resentful that Douglas should have thrust the fate of his brother so abruptly on him.

On the other hand it might just be that the man had an unfortunate personality, one of the ones who had suffered like Morton, who had sat with his blue pointed nose studying him so intently. Perhaps Morton was inventing the story about his brother. But he couldn't afford to assume that, he must investigate.

When he had eaten his food he walked in the direction Morton had told him. The condition of the houses deteriorated as he made his way along: it seemed to him that he was in an area which looked as derelict and abandoned as parts of Glasgow, before the rebuilding had started. He met a shoeless woman staggering along the street muttering to herself and later passed a spastic in a wheelchair who was holding out his hands for donations, a living advertisement for the cause which he in his helplessness represented. While he held the tin out his head and hands trembled uncontrollably. Trevor put a dollar in the tin and couldn't make out whether the movement of the head was a nervous tic or a nod of thanks. On the other side of the pavement he saw a pair of boys running past in ragged clothes. But these would only be isolated examples of deprivation, he thought, to be expected in a city of this size.

At last he found the house whose address Morton had given him, and this with much difficulty, for its number didn't appear in the regular order of street numbers but was in a small lane round a corner. The evening was very sultry and he felt that there was lightning and thunder imminent as on the night when he had travelled through Canberra in a taxi and had seen flashes of ghostly light on the horizon. He mopped his brow two or three times with his handkerchief and then rang the doorbell which was sunk in the stone at the side of an unpainted and scarred door. No one appeared and as he stood there in the silence looking around him it seemed to him suddenly that he was very vulnerable and open to attack. After a while when there was still no answer he went round to a window and could see through it a bare room in which there was only an old television set and a sink full of unwashed dishes. He went back to the door and rang the bell again and again there was no answer. Trembling, he pushed the door and it opened creakingly.

65

"Norman," he whispered from the dark hall, but there was no answer, and the house seemed both deserted and threatening. He entered a bedroom whose bare floorboards squeaked. A clock ticked on a wall above him, but of human presence there was no sign. There were no carpets on any of the floors, no pictures on the walls. On the kitchen table he found a blue ashtray crammed with cigarette ends. He felt a frightened intruder as he stood uncertainly in what appeared to be the living room, though it too was bare. From the dark tiny bathroom next door he heard the insistent monotonous dripping of water from a tap. Morton had clearly deceived him: either that or the owner had not returned, if he was indeed working. There was no sign of his brother's presence in the house at all.

Feeling more and more oppressed by a sense of danger he turned away from the living room and made for the main door. He tried to open it but couldn't. He tugged and tugged but couldn't move it. Was his mind playing tricks on him? On the other hand he could remember perfectly well leaving the door unlocked and in any case if it had been locked he wouldn't have been able to get into the house without a key. So there must be someone else with him in that house at that very moment, perhaps his brother, enraged and revengeful, watching him, stalking him. He waited, feeling his heart beat heavily and quickly. And then in the silence he heard the faint, almost inaudible squeak of a floorboard. He turned towards the window in panic. Perhaps he should smash a pane and get out that way, but his respect for property wouldn't allow him to do so.

He heard the squeak of the floorboard again. There definitely was someone in the house. He looked frantically around him for a weapon for he now knew with complete certainty that whoever was in the house was his enemy. Even if it was his brother, he was his enemy, too. But he could find no weapon anywhere, for the rooms were bare. And all the time he sensed a being stalking him, taking its time, patient and mocking, and yet in a curious way relentless.

"Who are you?" he shouted and his voice emerged as a thin, querulous scream.

"Who are you? I know there is someone there."

But there was no answer. Was it perhaps Morton who had followed him? Or was it his brother or the owner of the house? Or perhaps Douglas. He felt hostility in the air of the house, a scornful, insouciant ruthlessness as of someone waiting.

Again he shouted and again there was no answer, except for the deliberate squeak of a board. He knew that he was being tantalized, deliberately taunted.

Helplessly he stood in the living room. On the wall in front of him was a big mirror flecked with stains and dust. He stared intently at the reflection of his own face in the fading light. It looked gaunt and very frightened. The creaking had now stopped and there was a definite sense of approaching menace as if whoever it was who had been causing the creaking had tired of the foreplay. Fatefully, with a sort of heavy acceptance, he turned round and there was the man standing in the doorway smiling at him and then drifting towards him slowly as if in a ballet. Then Trevor was hit by a blow which felled him to the ground. Before he lost consciousness he felt hands scurrying about him, searching for his wallet, and knew that his money was gone.

Eight

WHEN HE WOKE up, the sun shining brightly in his eyes, he couldn't at first remember what had happened to him. He was staring up at what appeared to be a piece of statuary, alabaster legs, alabaster wings flowering from an alabaster body, an alabaster bow in the hand. There was grass under him and he could hear from somewhere the noise of water. He stared hopelessly up at the clouds that passed across the sky. He wanted not to get up, feeling that if he did so he would face a disaster so complete that he might not be able to survive it. And yet he must get up, he mustn't lie there. He must stand up and face whatever had happened to him. Nevertheless he closed his eyes briefly against the pain in his head, and still with his eyes closed touched the back of his head with his hand. He felt a crust there as if it were dry blood and when he removed his hand and looked at it there were small red flakes on it. Opening his eyes slowly again against the brightness of the sun, he levered himself from the ground and saw that he was beside a fountain and that the alabaster figure that he had seen earlier was a Cupid with a drawn bow, its hollow eyes staring upward, its body childlike and plump. At the same time he felt such a dreadful thirst that he began to drink greedily from the fountain while at the same time splashing water on his face and head. I must have been here all night, he thought; they, or he, must have taken me here and dumped me. He supposed that there must have been two people, not one: for all he knew one of them might have been his own brother. He passed his hand across his face and felt the stubble that had grown during his period of unconsciousness.

And then as he swayed by the fountain it came to him with a frightening shock that his wallet was gone. Very carefully and as if willing its reappearance he put his hand inside his breast pocket. The wallet wasn't there.

He stood there sweating profusely in the heat of the foreign sun trying to reassemble himself as if he were a piece of broken machinery. He was in Sydney and he had no money. What was he going to do? Could he sneak back to the hotel and take out his case without being seen? But then he had no money to pay his fare back to Canberra and couldn't find his return ticket which must also have been in his wallet. He tried his other pockets frantically but he could find nothing, he had been comprehensively robbed. Even his watch was gone from his wrist leaving a white band on the flesh, and he didn't even know what the time was. He felt naked and trembling and panicky in the day. What if he couldn't get back to Canberra again, what if he had to stay in Sydney for the rest of his life? Who would lend him the money to return home (for he thought of Canberra as home)? Could he possibly ask the man in the hotel to phone on his behalf to Canberra? But then he didn't know the people in the bank very well nor did he know the professor well enough to ask him for money. And what would the latter think of his grimy, surrealistic story?

So this was what it was like to be destitute in a world that didn't owe one a living, that was in the end merciless and glaring and indifferent. So this was what it was like to be totally on one's own.

He felt in his breast pocket again as if it were possible that he had made a mistake, that his wallet was there after all, but there was no doubt about it, it had irretrievably gone. He didn't even feel anger against those who had robbed him, it was as if from the moment that he had left Canberra this state of destitution had been predetermined.

The world was immense and pitiless around him and even now his attitude towards the people he saw walking down the street had changed; they seemed to him to belong to a world different from his own. Nevertheless he couldn't stand there all day, he must act. If he couldn't do something soon he might remain passively there forever. Money, that was what he needed. Thank God he had been careful enough to leave his passport in his case in his room in Canberra: at least he hadn't lost that. He looked down at his arms which were swollen and red with raw weals and then at his trousers which had lost their crease and looked rumpled. One of the worst things that had happened was the disappearance of his watch: without it he felt naked and disoriented. He stared down at the pale band which its removal had left on his arm: it was like the mark you saw when you lifted a stone and peered underneath it.

Still slightly unsteady on his feet, he left the fountain and began to walk away from the park and it was as if he was leaving behind him a refuge. People walked up and down the street staring straight ahead of them. He felt that he must appear stripped and dispossessed, but no one took the slightest notice of him. Ahead of him he could see the door of his hotel but he didn't want to go through it. He tried to think if there was any money in his case and then remembered that there

70

wasn't. Why had he been such a fool as to carry so much money on his person? Or why hadn't he converted his money into travellers' cheques? But it was too late now.

And then he stopped and considered. An idea came to him. Would it not be the best thing to go to the Salvation Army office and see that woman Mrs Tennant and ask for a loan till he got back to Canberra? Alternatively he might go to the police and report his loss. But some instinct made him decide against that. If he went to the police they might make him stay in Sydney while they questioned him. He simply wished to get out of Sydney and go back to his own room in the college: his mind ached with the desire to do so. He thought of Canberra and not Glasgow as his home.

As he made his way towards the Salvation Army offices, he no longer worried about his brother: his more immediate concern was to save his own skin. Had he not done enough? What more could be expected of him? Anyway he no longer believed that his brother was alive and if he was he couldn't be in any worse condition than he was himself. Thinking these thoughts he found himself at his destination. He stood in front of the window of a shop and tried to straighten his tie. Then very slowly he climbed the stairs to the office.

Mrs Tennant was there, matronly, composed and calm.

"Mr Grierson," she said in surprise. "I'm sorry but we don't have any more news."

He stared at her, at first unable to speak. Then he said, speaking very carefully, for he found that his voice was actually trembling.

"I came to ask you for money."

He tried to smile in a civilized manner as if he was making a joke but the muscles of his face were stiff.

"I went to a Home that Douglas told me about and when I

was in a house to which I was directed by an inmate I was hit over the head. My wallet was stolen, all the money I had. Can you give me some money to take me back to Canberra? I would repay you, naturally.''

"What?'' she said. "You were beaten up. You must inform the police at once.''

"No,'' he said, "I don't wish to do that. All I want is to get back to Canberra. I'm tired of all this. I don't know what's been happening to me since I came to Sydney.''

"I think first of all you should have a cup of tea,'' she said, briskly efficient. "I'll ring.'' She did so and when a young girl came into the office she asked if she could bring some hot sweet tea through.

"Now tell me what happened,'' she said, when the girl had gone.

"I went along to that Home,'' said Trevor. "I met a man there and he told me that he knew my brother. He sent me along to another house.''

"Have you got the address?''

He put his hand into his pocket without thinking and then recollecting what had happened to him said, "How stupid of me. I'm afraid I haven't, I had it on a piece of paper in my pocket. I certainly don't want to go back there.''

"I think you should report this to the police. Shall I do it?''

"No I won't bother. I still have my passport and my air ticket back to Glasgow. I don't want to stay here in Sydney. I want to go back to Canberra.'' The image of his brother which had once shimmered like a mirage in a desert had now faded from his mind.

"Are you feeling all right?''

"Yes, I'm feeling all right. Just a little pain in my head but it will go away. I'm angry at my own stupidity. I shouldn't have

72

listened to that man, who told me about my brother. Can you give me enough money to pay my bus fare back to Canberra? That's all I need. Of course it would only be a loan.''

"Of course I can loan you the money," she said.

"I shall send it back," Trevor insisted. "I shall definitely send it back. If you will give me the address of this office. I've got money in the bank in Canberra. You've been very good to me."

She handed him 30 dollars and a card with the address.

"That should be enough," she said. "But what about meals?"

"I don't want a meal," he said. "All I want is enough money to pay for the bus. I shall stay in the hotel till near the time the bus leaves."

He drank the sweet tea which the young girl had brought in. The panic and the fear were beginning slowly to dissipate.

"For a moment there," he told Mrs Tennant, "I felt what it must be like to be alone in the world. Do you understand?" She nodded wordlessly, but it was as if she didn't really understand, and he had a compulsion to speak.

"It was as if there was no one in the world but me, and I saw everything clearly and it was all hostile." It occurred to him that if she really understood what he was trying to say she wouldn't be able to do the job that she was doing.

"I could have stopped a stranger in the street and asked him for money," he said, hardly believing his own words but knowing that they were true.

"I understand," said Mrs Tennant, out of her massive calm, "now drink your tea."

"I felt surrounded by enemies," Trevor insisted, "a blankness came over me. I can't tell you what it was like." He stared down at his unpolished shoes.

"What should I do with the dollars?" he asked helplessly. "I might be attacked again."

"I don't think that will happen," she said briskly. "But if you like I could send someone to collect your ticket."

"No, no, that won't be necessary. It's daylight now. I shouldn't think they'll attack me in daylight on a busy street."

"I still think you should phone the police."

"And be kept in Sydney for days? No. In any case, I don't have any witnesses to what happened. It was a man called Morton from that Home who sent me to the house where I was attacked: he said that my brother lived there. I don't know whether he lived there or not. I don't know where he is. I'm sure now that he's dead. I feel it."

"I don't think he is," said Mrs Tennant quickly. "Someone tried to take advantage of you, that's all. They realized you were a stranger in the city. It has nothing at all to do with your brother."

"Well, I had better not keep you any longer," said Trevor. "You have a great deal to do." And indeed she was beginning to look rather impatient and he sensed that her hand was itching to use the phone, to continue her practical pursuits. And even as he had finished speaking the phone rang. She picked it up and while she was speaking into it he got to his feet and left the room, waving to her as he went out the door. He descended the stairs keeping his hand in the pocket where the dollars were. Should he keep them in his back pocket or in one of his side pockets? The question troubled him as he made his way along to the hotel.

He stood for a while facing its blank, scarred door. He didn't want to go in. He thought of the rickety lift, the negro he had glimpsed momentarily in the corridor. And then he suddenly remembered that his bill had already been paid. Why hadn't he remembered before? All he had to do was go to his room, remove his case and make his way towards the bus station. He would stay there all day if necessary till a bus left: he wouldn't stay in the hotel after all. The idea of finally leaving the hotel was so joyful that he decided that he would not take the lift but descend by the stairs instead. And then as he reached his room he suddenly realized that the key, which he had had in his pocket, was also gone. He stood outside, almost weeping with rage and frustration and feeling pity for himself. He would have to go to see the owner or manager whose office was on the sixth floor, and he would have to take that lift again — that creaking, superannuated coffin — and explain that he had lost his key.

As he walked along the corridor towards the lift he saw a boy and girl come out of a room hand in hand. In the light of the day they appeared harmless enough, laughing and chattering, their faces turned radiantly towards each other. Why, then, had he thought that this hotel was dangerous and evil?

When he reached the sixth floor he found the swarthy-faced man he had met before, sitting behind his desk as previously.

"I'm sorry," said Trevor hesitantly. "I'm afraid I've lost my key. I don't know what happened to it, and now I've locked myself out."

"Oh, that's all right," said the man, "no worries." It happens all the time. I'll come down with you." They took the lift down together, Trevor not speaking.

"You see, I have a master key," said the man.

They walked along the corridor side by side and when they reached Trevor's room the man opened it for him.

"There you are," he said. "I'll get another key made. You're not leaving for another four days, are you?"

"No," said Trevor, guilty at having to lie.

"Just pull the door behind you," said the man. "I'll get another key made for you. When will you be back in again?"

"Oh, about nine or ten," said Trevor quickly. "I might go to the cinema or the theatre. Thank you very much. It's very good of you."

He felt he ought to give the man a tip but at the same time he didn't know how much money he could afford, and would need for the bus. So he stood there awkwardly outside the door till the man had gone away. After all he had been kind, and it might have been a mosquito, not fleas, which had made his arms come out in red weals. He felt he ought to apologize to the man but by the time he had thought of doing so the lift was climbing creakily towards the sixth floor. If he had had arrived earlier on the first night he might not have had such a bad impression of the hotel.

He entered the room, pulling the door shut behind him. He examined it minutely, thinking that someone might have been there in his absence, but it looked undisturbed. The bed had been made, and looked clean and tidy. Though the harsh sunlight showed the scars and spots and stains which discoloured walls and ceiling and furniture there was, he now thought, a plain honesty about the room, and it appeared cleaner than he had remembered it. He lay on the bed and stared up at the ceiling with its diseased galaxy. I could stay here forever, he thought, I could lie here and do nothing. I could remain protected and sheltered here if I had enough money to pay for my hotel. He didn't want to go into the city again, into its noise and its terrors. He felt himself falling asleep in the serene light of the sun. I mustn't do that, he thought, and got up from the bed with a brisk movement. He put his things back in the case and decided that he must shave. There was no mirror in the room and he forced himself to go next door to the bathroom. After he had shaved he almost ran back into his bedroom again.

All the time he was in the bathroom he didn't want to lock the door in case someone might surreptitiously go into his room which he had left unlocked. He also wore his jacket even while he was shaving, and when he had finished, checked that he had his 30 dollars safe in his pocket. After entering the bedroom again he put his shaving gear into his case along with the rest of his things and zipped it shut. He peered out into the corridor, and then, walking quickly along it, tiptoed down the stair. All the time he was walking he was afraid that a voice would shout to him to come back: but after all he was doing nothing wrong, he had paid for his room. Yet he seemed to hear a voice saying to him: Your brother. What have you done with your brother? You're leaving him behind you. You're running away from him. Perhaps Norman had once slept in that bed he had just left, shaved in that yellowing basin. Perhaps he too had lain on the bed and stared up hopelessly at the ceiliing, at the constellation of brown stains. He opened the door, case in hand, and stepped out into the bright sunshine again. He felt that he would never return safely to Canberra, that someone evil and unscrupulous was waiting for him. I won't take a taxi, he thought, I'll walk now to the bus station and wait there all day if necessary.

As he was walking along by the side of the park he saw a bald man lying on the grass, beside him an empty wine bottle which reflected the sun. It seemed to him that it was the same man as he had seen the day before and that he had not shifted his position since, as passive as an inanimate object, such as a boulder. On an impulse he walked over and stood there looking down at him. The man was facing downward, and all that Trevor could see was his neck, which was brown and creased and tanned with the sun. His right hand was flung out carelessly from him. It seemed to Trevor for a moment that he was dead, he could see no sign of breathing. Perhaps he had been lying there dead since yesterday and nobody had noticed him. He bent down to try and see his face, as if it was perhaps Norman, and he had to identify him. He didn't want to touch the man though he could see now that he was breathing. His brother, like himself and this man, had shown signs of approaching baldness in his youth: and now he might not even know him. He bent down lower and lower, keeping his hand in his pocket where his dollars were. But all he could see was the brown neck and the right ear and the legs in their broken boots. If he had had money he would have left some with him, perhaps laid it beside him on the dry grass, but then he decided that it couldn't be his brother, that would be too great a coincidence. Suddenly, as if sensing his presence with the supernatural alertness of an animal, the man turned on his back and looked straight up at Trevor, revealing an unshaven face bloated and red with drink. Trevor smelt quite palpably the stench of alcohol pouring from him like a wind of ill omen. The yellow teeth glared as the man smiled a broken smile, a knowing leer, and one of the eyes winked at Trevor. In a terror greater than he had ever known he ran along the road past the classical fountain where the plump, blank-eyed Cupid aimed his bow out of the transparent umbrella of water, while the man, now leaning on his elbow, followed him with his red-veined eyes and made as if to shout, his obscenely naked head shining in the sun like a tomato. Trevor ran along the pavement with his case.

Nine

ARRIVED AT THE bus station he bought himself a ticket and sat down in one of the deep black leather chairs. A bus would be leaving at three o'clock, he was told. He bought himself some newspapers and magazines and read them voraciously one after another, satisfying some desperate hunger, while at the same time he protected the ticket which he had put in his right-hand pocket. He had a feeling that he would never get out of Sydney, that some new disaster would happen to prevent him from doing so, that perhaps his ticket might be stolen. He had already lost at least two hundred dollars in cash.

"No worries," the man at the counter had said to him when he had enquired about the bus. "There's plenty of room." Yet it seemed to him that he was running away though he didn't know what else to do to find his brother. Had he not tried his best? How could he be expected to do more? Nevertheless, as he sat there reading his paper the image of his brother's face shimmered in front of him.

"No I don't have any money," he pleaded with it as if he were in a courtroom. "I can't do any more."

He read in one of the papers that the body of a man had been found in Sydney Harbour. What if it was his brother? What if Douglas had been watching him all the time, sending him on this journey so that he himself could find Norman and settle some obscure business with him? He kept his case between his legs while people sat beside him and left to be replaced by others. If only he had kept contact with Norman all those years, if he had not been so totally absorbed in himself. Australia had become to him a frightening country on which his brother's face was painted over and over as if by a surrealist artist. The bareness of the country was making him confront all that he was. He remembered a painting he had seen by Nolan of two explorers riding on camels through a brown desert, one turned round on his horse and facing the spectator, wearing glasses, and appearing totally out of place in that landscape to which camels were native, the colour of the sand around them.

When it was time to leave he had to walk towards the bus as if into a high wind. He put his case on the rack and sat in a seat at the back. He felt a deep desire to sleep and yet had a feeling that he would be unable to do so. None of the people who had been travelling with him to Sydney was on his bus. In the seat across the aisle there was a boy with one arm in plaster and in front of him there were two women in flowery hats. As the bus made its way through one of the desolate areas of Sydney he looked through the window at the bluish houses — coloured thus by the perspex as if they belonged to the sky rather than to common earth — and thought of the heaven offered by the religionists, according to Marx. Blue clothes lines with blue ragged clothing hung in the blue calm day. Then they were out of Sydney and heading for Canberra on the open road. The landscape was as dry as ever for mile after mile. How different it was from the green landscape of home, with its mountains and glens and water. Yet it seemed to him that this dry landscape also corresponded with some deep dryness in his own heart, some sterility, a lack of simple feeling, of passion. Why had he not phoned Sheila yet to tell her of what had happened? Was there some fracture in their marriage? Surely he would have phoned her otherwise. Sheila, of course, was very different from himself: why, she would cry when she saw certain films on television. She would also rant and shout shamelessly at him. He himself no longer had this primitive strength of feeling. He didn't even seem to feel anger any more: his heart had become an almost stony thing. He took out a magazine and read an article on unemployment, then one on Afghanistan. Then he read a story which said that America had asked Australia whether she would stop her grain exports to Iran. In the end, everything was economic. Why had he himself not sent money to his brother? If someone had asked him to evaluate what had happened in Iran or Afghanistan he would have set down the arguments side by side and his conclusions would have been on the basis of the mind alone. Would it not be better to be a fanatic than to feel nothing? Would it not be better to kill in rage and pride than to be a stone?

The women in front of him were talking to each other. One was saying, "My husband couldn't come with me this time, we couldn't afford the air fares for the two of us. But I wanted to see my daughter. He understands that."

And the other one said, "It's eight hundred pounds now, the fare, isn't it?"

The bus sped on while the driver played cassettes of pop music including 'Bridge Over Troubled Water', and, later, 'Send In The Clowns'. The driver didn't brake at the corners but accelerated through them. So far Trevor hadn't seen any sign which said 'Canberra' though he had seen plenty for Melbourne. It was as if he was more homesick for Canberra than he was for Glasgow. He could not be happy till he was ensconced in his own room, till he got back to his usual routine.

Australia was such a vast place. It was the land of birds that couldn't fly, of animals that hopped like birds. It was a land of halted evolution. It was a land of jails and mates and the beguiling koala. It was a land where women were all called sheilas. He remembered the day he had visited the War Museum and had seen a diorama of Australian troops searching a village in Vietnam. He remembered the film *Apocalypse Now* which he had seen in one of the cinemas. The hero had travelled upriver into the deserts of himself to find a madman who had created his own personal inferno, skulls that dumbly ringed a jungle glade, row on row, circle on grinning circle.

When he reached Canberra he would phone Douglas and find out exactly what was going on, but from his own ground, from Canberra, from the place where he felt most secure. If only his brother had left Sydney and had found himself a small, undemanding place! The endless road unwound before him, taking him further and further away from Norman. He had a panicky feeling that he should get off the bus and return to Sydney. He looked down to see what time it was and saw the white, naked band on the wrist where the watch had been. He would have to buy a new watch. And yet there was no one he could tell his story to. How could he tell it to Professor Hastie who would wonder what sort of relatives he had? No, he couldn't tell him, and he didn't even want to tell Sheila. It was a secret that he would have to keep with him so long as he lived, and the loss of his brother would be a doom on his heart. The smiling face under the diced cap of the Argylls smiled at him from the blue window (the sky that travelled with him) and he shut his eyes against it. He felt as if he was going to faint.

The bus sped on. On both sides of him was the monotonous, unforgiving landscape which hadn't tasted rain for months and on which the sun beat down day after day. His own days were now like that. In his work in Glasgow University his life had been a bookish routine, and now when that routine had been broken so brutally he couldn't cope. His failure irritated him as if it was of the deepest significance. If he didn't have the integrity to search for his own brother what did his lecturing signify. CALL IN AT JANET'S said a sign over a shop. I AM SAILING, said the voice on the cassette.

How alone he had always been: he had no close friends at all. In this land of mateship he was a solitary. His brother had always made friends more easily than he. Why, when Norman was visiting their cousin he would go over to the food cupboard and help himself to food without asking. He himself didn't have that spontaneity and never would have. The cousin loved Norman for it. His brother, in fact, was a better human being than himself, his generosity had flowed easily from him without calculation. He himself, on the other hand, always inspected experience very closely before using it and thus continually infected it with self. He closed his eyes, pitying himself for his isolation in this immense burgeoning land, for the fact that when he had been asked for the colour of his brother's eyes he had hesitated. Suddenly he slept.

When he woke up the sky was darkening and there were lights in the town which he passed. He peered forward and saw that they were only 50 kilometres from Canberra. He

83

tried to remember how one converted kilometres to miles but couldn't. The two women in front of him were still talking and the boy with the arm in plaster was lolling against his seat half-asleep. When he arrived in Canberra he would take a taxi to the college, he still had enough money for that. He saw a glare on the horizon signifying a city and thought it might be Canberra but wasn't sure. He tried to read the papers he had bought but found that it was too dark to do so. It was funny that the light on these buses was so low but that might be because the distances were so much greater than in Scotland and the passengers might wish to sleep. Through the window he could see a moon, small and shrunken, and white in the sky, like a curved bone, ancient and aboriginal, and far from the main road he could see the twinkling lights of farmhouses. In another fifty years perhaps these vast spaces would be populated and Australia would no longer be what it was now, a huge land almost empty of people, except in the cities.

The boy with the arm in plaster suddenly woke up like an embalmed corpse taking on life, stared wildly about him and then pretended to examine his plaster which was scribbled over with names. An old man with a pointed beard, scholarly as a rabbi, gazed steadily ahead of him and for a moment Trevor was reminded of the German professor who sat by the pool in the college grounds studying Heine. He too had a pointed beard and seemed to read steadily all day, sitting on his frail black chair among the orange leaves of autumn while the black cat with the four new kittens prowled restlessly for birds. He tried to remember the professor's name but couldn't. They passed each other every day but with the tense self-consciousness of scholars, used more to the study than the open air, didn't speak.

There was no question about it, he had failed in his mission, he had come home with his tail between his legs, he was so frightened of what might happen to himself that he had to give up on a quest that might prove more important to him than life itself, or at least as important.

The bus careered on through the night, the driver probably wanting to go home to his wife and children. And now they had entered Canberra and he could see the landmarks by which he usually guided himself. Surely that was the Lakeside Hotel towering into the air. And that other building shaped like a bulbous minaret, what was the name of that? The ordered city met him with its ordered lights. The bus drew up at the bus station. People all began to prepare to leave it as if they were corpses wakening from the dead. He himself rushed forward to the door, and looked around him for taxis, and there they were waiting. He flagged one and climbed into it. He gave the driver the name of the college and sat in the back seat. Perhaps he should have sat in the front seat: Australia was the land of equality. Perhaps the driver wished to speak but he himself didn't want to; he felt exhausted. He watched with joy as they wound their way between the trees, past the colourful bushes, as they passed buildings on which ancient ivy grew.

When they pulled up at the door of the college he gave the driver three dollars for his fare, and an extra one as a tip. He took his case and made his way to his room as if he were rushing into hiding, into a hermitage. He was about to unlock the door when he suddenly realized that he had lost his key to this place as well. Why hadn't he thought of that, and why hadn't he remembered to hand it in when he had left? And he cursed feebly the bitter injustice of the world. He went along to the office hoping that it was still open. The girl at the desk told him that she would try to find a key and he waited idly, watching a beautiful, elegant Japanese woman who was standing in the hall reading advertisements and posters about classical concerts and films. After a long while the girl returned and gave him a key. He turned away from the office with its slits for internal and external mail; its alarm clock lying on the desk, blank-faced and distant. He walked past the common-room where a Chinaman was standing reading a newspaper. He heard the noise of the television and saw its blue light as he passed the television room: it seemed to him that the programme was *Fawlty Towers*. He climbed the stair to his room and inserted the key in the lock. His own tables and chairs struck out at him like a blow. The room looked suddenly bare and forlorn, scantily furnished, and the books seemed to belong to someone else. He shut the door behind him and sat down on a chair like an exhausted boxer. Through the window he could see the vague white trees, trunks of the eucalyptus, ghostly in the night. He felt that this place was no longer his secret home, but rather a precarious shell floating in the darkness. Through the quietness he heard a flute being played with delicate embroidered cadences. Below him in the gathering dimness he could see the tables and seats where people would often sit till late at night clinking glasses and laughing boisterously. He saw on the table in his own room the exercise book containing the notes that he had been writing and they appeared ineffectual and senseless. He opened the partition which shut off the living room from the kitchenette and poured himself a huge whisky which he drank in one gulp.

About an hour later and befuddled with drink he took off his clothes and ran a bath. His arms were still inflamed and red and swollen with weals. He got into the bath and cleaned himself thoroughly seeing, floating on the water, black flecks like the bodies of dead fleas. It was as if he was washing himself free of all the dirtiness and sordidness of Sydney and by doing so liberating himself from his perplexities. After he had let the water run away and rinsed the bath he locked the door of the bedroom from the inside, frightened that perhaps someone would come in and attack him in his sleep. He looked down into the garden past the wire mesh that protected the window. There was here no whine of mosquitoes or other insects, there was only the silence of the night interrupted by the wavering notes of the flute. It reminded him momentarily of the sweet, forsaken notes of a bugle.

Pain twitched at the corner of his mouth and he slept.

Ten

TREVOR LISTENED TO Professor Anderson talking about Richardson, noticing that on the table there were the usual glasses of wine and orange juice. There were perhaps 25 people in the room altogether, arranged in a semi-circle around the professor who was reading from a sheaf of type-script. He himself had never managed to study much of Richardson but remembered him as an author of novels in which a member of the upper classes, usually a squire, tried to seduce a maidservant, usually obsessed with sexual prudery, into bed with him. The professor was talking about the devices used to prolong suspense in the author's long epistolary novels and how in one of the books Richardson had great difficulty with the ending.

For the first time since he had come to Australia Trevor felt restless, imagining himself, inside the room with the other lecturers and professors, as a goldfish in a pond such as the one that adjoined the college. Everything around him was clean and hushed and polished, though now and again when he remembered the weals on his arms he shivered with dis-taste and shame. It seemed to the professor, as far as Trevor could make out, that Richardson was a greater novelist than Fielding since he had been so winding and oblique and experimental in a curiously modern psychological manner. He noticed that the German professor was writing furiously in a notebook, his hair falling over his eyes, preparing himself to deliver a learned fusillade of questions at the end of the lecture. He felt at the same time a drilling ache beginning to throb relentlessly behind his right eye, as if a needle were being inserted there. Hadn't Douglas said that he suffered frequently from headaches? He had a picture of the leering squire bending over the apparently innocent yet calculating servant girl in the middle of a rural night impregnated with the scents of blossoms. The lecturer had made a joke and the German professor laughed before anyone else did, like an obedient and perceptive pupil. Suddenly Trevor couldn't stand being there any longer and rose quickly and left the room, making a muttered apology as he passed the lecturer.

He walked along a corridor and saw a telephone there. He took some cents from his pocket and dialled the number which Douglas had given him. The phone rang endlessly, perhaps in an empty house. Where on earth was Douglas? Why did he never answer?

He left the college and walked into Canberra, passing some beautiful trees with orange leaves on the way, while under them some students were reading quietly in a tranquil Arcadia of their own. For a brief moment his university days returned to him, piercing and present, in a fresh poignancy of feeling. Then he remembered quite out of the blue that Australians were compelled to vote and unless they did so they were fined. He made his way to the post office and asked if he could see the voting registers. But if Douglas had only been in Canberra a short time his name might not be on the register. He looked up the name DOUGLAS but could find only three and none of them had the initials that he had been given.

When he came out of the post office he didn't know what to do next. He had no address for Douglas and he felt helpless and baffled. He sat down on a green bench beside a tramp who had a bag at his feet and as before he watched a small bird pecking at crumbs which had been thrown to it by passers by. It occurred to him that its fierce dedication to the moment wouldn't allow it to comment on its surroundings even if it wished to do so: birds couldn't be poets, however lyrical for instance nightingales might appear in mythology. Prose, poetry, these were the luxuries of a mind which preyed on landscapes and people, freed from economic necessity. A fountain jetted clear water into the sparkling air. A man was talking into a microphone about the Fraser Government, attacking it for its right-wing policies that were causing so much unemployment. All around him he could see the privileged, well-dressed people in an arcade that had beautiful shops.

Feeling suddenly disgusted with his own idleness, he walked back to the college again, as if he were hurrying to a specific destination. He didn't know what he would do if Douglas didn't communicate with him. He passed a police station and nearly went in to ask if they knew anything about Douglas, if they had his name on their books, but decided against it. There would have to be too much explanation, too much documentation, too much questioning. He turned towards his college and stood for a moment, before turning in, staring down at some ants which were scurrying across the dusty earth with their burdens of twigs. Even when they bumped into each other with obsessive haste they did not stop but continued on their relentlessly urgent journeys which to him appeared so mysterious.

He went to his room and lay down on the bed, then phoned Douglas again. Again the phone rang and rang with the same hollow sound, and no one answered. Had Douglas by some final black joke given him the number of a public call box and was the phone ringing perhaps at the side of a road somewhere? He looked down into the garden below at the red chairs, hearing from them the sound of laughter as people ate and drank from the wooden tables set in front of them. Such a simple almost bucolic scene! It seemed to him like a theatre readying itself for a great invisible event. The sprinklers played over the dusty earth in remorseless shining arcs and among the trees he saw a black cat loping silently, now and again stopping and gazing up into the trees where birds with brilliant plumage were perched like unattainable fruit.

Again he phoned and again there was no answer. He poured himself a whisky and lay on the bed watching the ceiling. He felt sleepy, and did not wish to continue with the notes of the lecture he had been preparing before he had left for Sydney. Then suddenly the phone rang stridently and he picked it up quickly. A voice at the other end said,

"Is that Mr Grierson?"

"Here," he said eagerly.

"This is Malcolm Douglas," said the voice. "You're back from Sydney? Did you find out anything?"

"I did," said Trevor. "Could I see you?"

"When?"

"Well, could you come here or could I go and see you?"

Douglas hesitated for a moment and then said, "You could come here, I suppose," and gave him an address

91

which Trevor copied down furiously on to the back of a page of his lecture notes.

"On the other hand," he said, "it might be more convenient for you to come here."

"It doesn't matter," said Douglas. "Whatever you want. You can come here if you wish."

"All right," said Trevor. "I'll come and see you. I've got a lot to tell you. When should I come?"

"Would you like to come tonight?" said Douglas.

"Yes, of course. I shall be there fairly soon." And then inconsequentially he added, "Which part of Scotland did you originally come from?"

"Ayrshire."

Trevor wanted to continue speaking, as if Douglas were his only link with reality but couldn't think of anything to say to him. Other people could chatter on about nothing in particular but he couldn't.

"All right then," he ended lamely. "I'll be along about half-past seven. Is that okay?"

"Yes," said Douglas. "No worries."

When he had put the phone down Trevor finished his whisky and then restlessly switched on the radio. A woman was interviewing someone about unemployment.

"Have you got much to live on?" she asked. Trevor switched the radio off and went out to the balcony. As he looked down on the lawn where the men and women were drinking and laughing he felt isolated and without energy. It seemed to him that the scene below him, the people, the trees, and the black cat were assembled into a drama of which he himself was the author. The flute player was still composing his watery notes, bubbling over a dry landscape. Many of the leaves were falling from the trees, and lying

92

on the lawn in yellow patterns.

He sat there for a long time and then decided that he ought to bring something to Douglas. Would a bottle of wine be sufficient? And what about the wife and child? He went down to the shop which adjoined the college and bought a flagon of white wine with the remains of the money that he had left over from the bus fare. He realized that he had forgotten to go to the bank and explain what had happened to him in Sydney and he cursed himself for his forgetfulness. Still, he had some money in his case which he could use. Feeling more restless than ever he decided that he could walk to the bank, which was in the city centre.

He took his passport out of his case and pulled the door shut behind him. He would need some money for the taxi that would take him to Douglas's house. He walked briskly out of the college again as if he had a renewed purpose in life, hoping that the people in the bank wouldn't be too officious. It seemed to him that his life which had been ordered had now become disordered. How had he not thought about the bank when he had been downtown before? Why, when he had come over to Australia he had written in a notebook all the places he would visit, and the dates in which he would be in those places. It was in fact lucky for him that he had thought of locking his passport and air ticket in his case when he had gone to Sydney. In that sense he had been more fortunate than he had deserved. He mopped his face with his handkerchief as he walked along, removing his jacket and carrying it over his arm, and making sure that his wallet wouldn't fall out.

He remembered, when the plane had landed briefly in the damp heat of Singapore, seeing a native lying under the shadow of the wing of a huge plane as if to protect himself from the intense humid heat: and later how some natives with their names written on the backs of their shirts had entered the plane to clean it. They talked to each other in their own language, which of course he hadn't understood. He had wondered vaguely what sort of life they led. Why, they were like servants attending to transient overlords, vassals to the aristocracy of the sky. And then the plane was airborne and they were heading into the sun and as the blinds were down because of the film that was being shown the windows suddenly became like the windows of a cathedral, encrusted with a blood-red colour. Down below were the fields which looked exactly like strips of linoleum or marquetry, wooden barren floors. And in the sea were boats with strangely shaped sails. Now the strangeness returned to him as if it had some deep significance.

Eleven

———————

AT A QUARTER-PAST seven he took a taxi from the college
to the address which Douglas had given him and which was
in Melba. It occurred to him that he wasn't as nervous now as
he had been in Sydney, as if the city of Canberra itself,
bureacratic, governmental, guaranteed order, though of
course this might be an illusion. He tried to speak to the taxi
driver who was unaccountably silent, and then gave up and
looked out of the window. It disturbed him a little that the
taxi driver didn't seem to know where the street was, and
had in fact taken out a map which he unfolded and studied
while the cab was standing at the traffic lights. At last he
found the street on his map and they sped on. Lights twin-
kled all over the city making it lustrous and beautiful.

At last the taxi stopped at No. 158 Morgan Close, though
the number Trevor wanted was 154. He told the taxi driver
that he would find the house himself and went to see whether
154 was two doors down from 158. It turned out however
that 157 was next to 158. As he searched for the house the
rain began to fall heavily and he sheltered under the over-
hanging roof of a tin hut, hearing the heavy drops banging

above him like hailstones. The houses didn't seem to be in a good area and he asked a fat woman who was puffing her way up a brae in the rain where 154 was. She pointed down the hill to another row of houses. The raindrops bounced from the road and in the distance he saw sheet lightning illuminating the sky. There were dull, hollow bursts of thunder.

He made a rush for the houses which she had indicated and as he ran along a pathway he saw Douglas standing at a window looking out. He knocked on the door and after a while Douglas came to it.

"Did you have difficulty finding the house?" he asked Trevor, whose jacket had been drenched by the rain.

"Yes," said Trevor angrily.

"My wife and child are out," Douglas told him, ignoring the fact that he looked enraged. The room into which Trevor was led seemed to be reasonably well furnished with black leather armchairs, and paintings on the walls. One of the paintings showed a face red as the sun resting on spindly legs, and its savage, almost primitive colouring made him wonder once again if there was something psychologically wrong with Douglas. The latter appeared tense and smoked continually.

They sat down opposite each other and Douglas said, "What did you find out then?"

Trevor told him everything that had happened to him and Douglas listened intently though rather impatiently, smoking furiously.

He didn't seem to have much sympathy for Trevor even when the latter told him that he had been hit on the head.

"That happens if you're not careful," he said. "Did you find out anything about Norman?"

"No," said Trevor. "I still don't know where he is."

"I'd better tell you what he told me," said Douglas at last. "You're not going to like this."

"Like what?"

"As I said, what Norman told me. I don't think you know him very well. That is my impression though I may be wrong. He's totally different from what you think he is. I imagine you consider him rather stupid because he didn't read books and left school early, but you would be wrong about that. Norman has worked out a technique for survival, you know. We all had to do that. I remember the time when we went to this particular place where they were giving out food. Do you know what we got? A pie each. They were practically uneatable. We hit rock bottom at that time. But we had a lot of fun too."

He went over to a cupboard and took out two cans of beer and opened them, ignoring the bottle of wine that Trevor had brought.

"You'll have one," he said. "I don't have very much money but I can run to beer."

Trevor who didn't usually drink beer accepted it just the same.

"I said you're not going to like this but Norman told me that when the two of you were growing up you were the one who was always getting preferential treatment. For instance you never took a job: you were studying for the university. Is that right?" And he lit another cigarette from the one he had just finished, drawing the smoke deeply into his lungs.

"He said that he started working after he left school but you were intended for university. One time when you were coming home from university he carried your case for you and he hurt his back. It was loaded with books. Do you remember that incident?''

''Yes.''

''That's what he told me. If there was any money for clothes it was you who got it; he didn't get any because he wasn't going to university. And when an uncle came home from Africa and he gave you five pounds for writing a letter for him you never thought of giving Norman any of the money. And at the time he was very short of money. He told me that he always regretted leaving school early.''

''What?'' said Trevor incredulously.

''That was what he said. But since you were getting all the preferential treatment he didn't think there was any point in staying on. As I told you, Norman isn't stupid. He may not appear to be paying much attention, but he doesn't miss much. He could have gone to university if he had wanted to. Psychologically your life depends on the way in which you are treated. You understand that. Have you read Laing?''

''Yes,'' said Trevor, ''I've read a little of him.''

''Well, then, you don't need me to tell you all this. My father came out here to join the Army but he didn't like it. To tell you the truth he had deserted from the British Army. He went back again to Britain and my mother divorced him. I was brought up by my mother: I can't remember my father very well. I can't take ordinary jobs because I get headaches. That is why I'm working on my novel. I'm sure it will be published: as I told you I have contacts.''

''I'm sure,'' said Trevor in an embarrassed manner.

''See, there you go again,'' said Douglas, who suddenly became very agitated. ''You're saying, 'I'm sure' when you don't mean it. You haven't seen my novel yet and you dismiss it. One thing that happens in publishing is that people lay down the law as to what you should accept as payment. I'll lay down my own rules: I'm not going to be tied to any publisher. Obviously publishers are going to look after themselves. Do you believe that?''

"I believe it," said Trevor, "but on the other hand if you're starting off for the first time . . ." And his voice trailed away.

"I'll do what I want," said Douglas, his uncertain temper flaring again. "Do you know what money I'm getting for my wife and child. Seventy dollars a week. The other night I couldn't type, the child was crying all the time. There's something rotten about this country. They say there is no class system but there is. We have a man in Queensland but I'd better not go on . . .' And he lit another cigarette, his hand shaking. "I told you I came from Ayrshire. My people were miners. They worked long shifts for little money. You wouldn't know about that. I'm sure that in your college there's plenty of food and wine."

"That's true," said Trevor, "but what I want to know is about Norman."

"I know you do and I'm coming to that. What seems to me fairly obvious is that you don't know anything about him. I know more about him than you seem to do. Don't worry about getting back," he told Trevor who was looking apprehensively through the window at the sheet lightning which played about the sky. "I'll phone for a taxi for you."

He paused and Trevor stared at him. The man was a tangle of nerves and rancour. He wondered how he could afford to smoke so many cigarettes on 70 dollars a week.

"Don't think I want money from you," said Douglas, "not at all. Have you ever heard of the cargo cult? The aborigines thought that supplies which came by plane

99

belonged to them because they came from the sky and there-
fore from their gods. They have a myth about a god who will
bring them food. I'm not like that. I don't have a myth like
that." It occurred to Trevor that this was a highly intelligent
man who had been almost crazed by destitution, but who
was still more penetrating and astute than he was himself.

"You see," Douglas continued, "you categorize people.
You probably think that your brother is an alcoholic and that
allows you to forget about him and think about alcoholism
instead. Everybody has a label for everybody else. When I
came back from Sydney my sister characterized me as the
black sheep. I don't speak to her now. What is an alcoholic?
Nobody knows. And they don't try to understand why each
individual became an alcoholic. Alcoholism is not like the
plague, it does not strike without reason. Perhaps your
brother Norman had the strength to break out of his environment, perhaps not. But he should not be characterized as an
alcoholic."

"But," protested Trevor, "alcoholism is a specific disease
which can be characterized."

Douglas became extremely agitated and walked about the
room smoking furiously.

"Not at all," he shouted. "And even if that were true
what would it tell us? What you have to do is to see your
brother as distinct from the disease. Do you understand me?
Perhaps that is what Christ did, though I'm not a Christian:
perhaps that is how he healed people." He smiled brilliantly,
exhaling smoke, and added, "You must read the literature
on this. I used to be a nurse in a hospital and I know it. I used
to be a psychiatric nurse."

"Was my brother being dried out then and were you
nursing him?" asked Trevor but Douglas didn't answer.

"I'll tell you," he said, "you still haven't changed. You have to learn more before you will be changed. I told you that you wouldn't like what I have to tell you." And he paused a long time as if collecting his thoughts. "You did a terrible thing to your brother, didn't you? In fact you are responsible for making him emigrate."

"Me?" said Trevor.

"When I met you you implied that he set off cheerfully for Australia as if it was a great adventure. These were your very words. Isn't that right?"

"I don't know whether I gave that impression or not," said Trevor.

"It wasn't an impression, it was a verbal commitment. You said that you saw him off. By this time he had finished his National Service. You gave the impression that he had been home for quite a long time. Perhaps two years."

"I don't . . ." Trevor began. But Douglas interrupted him.

"He wasn't home as long as two years at all," said Douglas. "He went away after a few months. He told me why he left and you don't need to disguise it any longer."

He paused and then began again, rubbing his forehead with his left hand as if he had another headache.

"What Norman told me was this. He had a girl friend when he went to the Army and at first she used to write to him. Her name was Sheila, by the way. He had met her at a dance. According to Norman she was very pretty." Trevor closed his eyes. Sheila had used to come and visit himself and his mother when his brother was in the Army. She was . . . it was true she was working in the same factory as his brother but at the same time she was ambitious and determined. Trevor had seen clearly what mettle she was made of but

101

Norman hadn't seen it at all. At first she would talk to the two of them and then one day he had taken her to the cinema, a matinée, he remembered. In the middle of the film, in the darkness, he had felt her hand in his, and he had looked at her, and then . . . All those years when he had been studying he had never gone with girls, he had been a monk resolute in the pursuit of knowledge. True, there had been one girl whom he had helped with her Virgil and another one who sporadically sent him a Christmas card . . . but that hadn't been serious.

Now it was as if a dam had burst and he had found himself in the presence of an experienced girl who knew how to use her sex as a weapon. He had never met anyone like her before, so compellingly demanding, so nakedly and practically intelligent and ambitious. Had it been love he felt for her? Surely it had been love. One night he had become embittered and jealous when she had danced too long with a friend of his, and he had been ashamed and confused and frightened. For never before in his whole life had he felt jealousy, the hunger for exclusive possession. That night he had dreamt a vivid dream. He was sitting in a room with a lot of people and a cat with enormous green eyes had appeared at the door staring at him, the eyes becoming more and more enlarged. He found himself humbly apologizing to her, presenting her with a bouquet of flowers at nine o'clock on the Saturday morning as if he were asking pardon from an empress. It was as if he was flayed and irrational, raw and torn. If it wasn't love, it was a sickness entirely foreign to his nature.

Many times he had tried to withdraw from her but found that he couldn't. She was, of course, two years younger than he was, the same age as Norman. They had gone for walks in the woods above the town, and there they had . . . He could at that very moment see the dapple of sunlight on the thick trunks of the trees, against one of which he had squeezed her in his desperation, as if he were nailing her to the wood, punishing her for his loss of innocence, for the green coolness that had forever left him.

When he thought of his brother he used to forgive himself because of the absolute helplessness of his condition. But should he not perhaps in all honour have emigrated instead of his brother? Shouldn't he have had the courage to take the absurd leap into the blue? There was the night he and Sheila had quarrelled in her sister's house because she was dancing alone on the floor, and he didn't like her dancing in front of other people.

"If you won't stop I'll leave you," he had said and had walked out into the frosty night. Half an hour later she had caught up with him in her sister's car as he plodded steadily towards the North Star.

"You know that I love you," she had said. But he didn't know. Why should she love him? He was bald, stupid, older than her. And why had she abandoned his brother so quickly?

One night she had told him, "I don't want to work in the factory for the rest of my days." Sometimes he felt barren and insecure but knew that he couldn't leave her. Though she had left school she was bright and sharp, and even tried to read some of the books he was reading. One night he had found her turning over the pages of a novel by Faulkner and was frightened by the pathos of the sight, for she was determined that she would read it through to the end. What else was that sickness but love?

They had discussions about whether they should tell his brother what had happened, for a letter from Norman

103

reached Sheila every week. "We won't tell him," she said, though his own instincts were to do so. She argued that he might do something silly, for after all he was very impulsive. But he who was so severely truthful wanted to tell him no matter what happened. He felt sordid and secretive and defiled. He wondered afterwards whether she was making sure that she would at least keep one or the other. "Eighteen months won't be long," she said, but at the same time she was making preparations for their wedding after Norman had come out of the Army. She showed him some clothes she had bought and she was also paying for a Hoover and washing machine. Her busy hopefulness was endearing: he felt himself surrendering more and more to her sense of purpose. He gave her money for furniture, in fact he was very generous with his money as if by denuding himself of it he was making a spiritual reparation. Not even his mother knew what was happening. Sometimes he used to think, "Perhaps she will meet someone else and she'll keep the washing machine and the Hoover which she has bought with my money." And it angered him that he should be so petty.

At night she would sit on the floor in her sister's house (the latter and her husband having gone out for the evening) and look up into his eyes in the light of the fire. There was nothing that he could refuse her and he felt proud that he had managed to ensnare someone who was so pretty and so young and so capable. In fact she was quite beautiful, though her nose was rather large and Caesarian and gave her a Roman appearance. She sometimes said that she would get a nose lift but he thought that she shouldn't in case she lost her look of busy determination. She would ask him what pay he would expect to get as a lecturer when he became one (and she was quite sure that he would).

"What are other lecturers' wives like?" she would ask him.

Trevor looked blankly into Douglas's face.

"The worst was," he said, "when Norman came home from the Army. He didn't know what had been going on. I can't tell you what Sheila had been saying to him in her letters, she never told me. One night we told him what had happened. He went dead white and then he left and ended up in a pub from which he came home late at night blind drunk." He paused. "My mother wondered what was wrong with him but I didn't tell her, and in spite of the fact that he was coming home drunk every night of the week I couldn't let Sheila go. I couldn't."

Sheila had been much stronger than him. "We can't allow this blackmail," she would say to him. "I'm not a piece of property. I've the right to change my mind if I want." Trevor thought that at one stage Norman would kill himself. But Sheila was much harder than he was. "He won't do anything of the kind," she said. What bothered him was that though he could see his brother so acutely in despair he couldn't leave Sheila. There was no chivalry left in his nature: the green cat had eaten all that up. He tried to many times, but couldn't. He had created quarrels, abdicated responsibility for the whole affair, claimed that it was Sheila who had seduced him, that it wasn't his fault, but at the end of the quarrels, when Sheila had threatened to leave both of them he had run after her and begged her forgiveness. Sometimes in the middle of the night he would waken up and feel a huge contempt for himself, as the dawn reddened the curtains.

"He won't speak to me at the factory," she had told

105

him. "It can't go on much longer." He thought that the whole thing would affect his results in the examinations but it didn't. He had passed with First Class Honours.

"You have all the luck," Norman had said to him, his eyes owlish with drink. His mother had objected to Trevor's marrying Sheila as well. "Can't you see? She's ambitious. That's why she left Norman." One night Norman had punched him in the face and he had accepted the punishment gratefully. His mother and Norman would quarrel and she would say,

"It's time you left here." She was as determined and strong as Sheila though in a different way. And yet she too was ambitious, had wanted a son who had attended university. The house seethed with unrest. Norman acquired the habit of sitting in front of the television set in such a way that Trevor couldn't see it: he was fertile with irritating tricks. But most of the time he himself had pitied Norman. The latter was one of the paupers of life. And yet he couldn't give up Sheila, and there was no point in doing so since she was determined to marry him and on no account would marry Norman. "It just shows you, all this drunkenness," she would say. "What would he have been like if I had married him? It's lucky that I found out in time." The statement seemed to Trevor sublimely irrational and he couldn't understand how Sheila's mind worked; she seemed able to convince herself of anything. It occurred to him that there was no truth in any idea as such: ideas conquer not because of their truth but because of the strength with which they are believed.

"It was me who should have emigrated," he told Douglas. "But I didn't have the courage. Do you understand?"

Douglas said nothing but lit another cigarette from the previous one and continued to smoke furiously, exhaling ring after grey ring. Trevor watched the frail circles with aesthetic detachment.

"The terrible thing was that I wasn't sure whether she loved me or not. Perhaps she did, does. And yet I haven't phoned her up since you told me about Norman. We married, of course."

"And?" said Douglas.

"I had to leave her behind, at home, but what is she doing now? I don't know. She keeps saying to me, 'You should be a professor and why aren't you? You let people walk all over you.' I remember the old places we used to go to when courting. There was one particular hill we used to sit on on the warm days. But she won't go near these places now. In fact one of the reasons why I came out here alone was to see if I could exist separated from her." He looked at Douglas with a naked defenceless stare. "I don't know what will happen if she leaves me. I don't suppose you have any whisky?" he asked hopefully.

"I'm sorry, it's too expensive. I can give you beer or wine. I don't drink much, as I told you."

Douglas poured some of the white wine that Trevor had brought into a glass.

"That's why when you phoned I didn't know what to do. I remember the day he left. He had been talking about emigrating for a while and I was only half listening. It came as a complete surprise when he said that he would be leaving on a particular day: he had secretly arranged his passport and everything. I don't want you there, he said, not any of you. Not even my mother. But we went just the same and we arrived at the pier just as the ship was leaving. There was a piper from the factory there, a fellow drinker he had become friendly with. Norman was wearing a kilt and making an exhibition of himself. I think he was drunk. The ship sailed away and I went into a pub and bought myself a drink.''

''And you never heard from him since?''

''He did write once or twice but only to his mother. He said things were going well with him. But he had no trade, you see. I don't know how they accepted him without a trade. He had only been working in a clock-making factory, as I told you. I came back drunk that day and Sheila was furious. 'I hope you're not going the same way as your brother,' she said. I stood looking at her and I thought, 'What have I done?' It was as if once my brother had gone there was no need for me to be with her any more. Maybe deep down I wanted to take her away from him for the sake of that itself. Who can understand the human mind? To take everything away from him so that he would be a beggar. Maybe I was punishing him. Do you think that's possible?''

''Yes.''

''What did you say?''

''I said yes.''

Trevor drained the wine and shifted restlessly in his chair. ''Of course we were always fighting when we were young. I have to try and tell you about Sheila. It's important.

''It turned out that she didn't love me at all. I think I can say that. She only wanted to get out of the house she was in. There were another three unmarried sisters and they quarrelled all the time. It was like a house full of cats, they fought and scratched each other without mercy. She told me that she knew that Norman wouldn't marry for years.

108

She told me that the factory was so boring that I couldn't imagine what it was like. And then again she thought that she would marry into a world where she would meet a lot of interesting people. In fact most of them are quiet and silent and immersed in their own projects, and they don't speak much to anyone. I brought a friend of mine to see her one night. He's a French lecturer and talked a great deal about existentialism. 'What a bore,' she said." Trevor stared dully ahead of him. "Do you understand what I'm saying?" he said. "It was all such a mess, such a tangle. And yet I was helpless."

There was a long silence and then Douglas said, "I have no wife or child. I can't afford them."

"What did you say?"

"You heard me. I have no family."

"But . . ."

"I simply told you that because you sounded so sure of yourself. On the radio."

"Oh. And did you ever meet my brother then?"

"Of course I did. I met him in a cheap lodging house. He was an alcoholic."

Trevor nearly said to him, "Why are you calling him an alcoholic when you said before that it is a simplistic label?"

"He told me that story," said Douglas, "or at least his own version of it. But he didn't know it as it really was. I can see that now. He was very embittered."

"But do you know where he is now?"

"No. That was years and years ago. It must have been fifteen years ago. No, perhaps ten. He had started to drink. That was in Queensland."

"But you said it was Sydney."

"No, it wasn't in Sydney."

"I see. And what about those books he was supposed to read?"

"He never read a book as far as I know. He looked sick."

"Sick?"

"Yes, he looked very sick. And then one day I heard your voice on the radio. I don't know who hit you on the head, by the way. It must have been that fellow Morton who saw a chance of getting money because you looked so green."

"I see," said Trevor. He felt as if he was rising and falling on a sea that was bitterly salt.

"Do you know anything about him now?"

"Not a thing."

"But why . . ." And his voice trailed away.

"I told you. You sounded so cocky."

The two of them, himself and Norman, were walking through a wood. He himself hid behind a tree and waited for his brother to try and find him. His name echoed among the trees which were dappled with sunlight. His brother was shouting that he was lost and he himself was smiling secretly. And now Douglas was doing the same thing to him.

"And your book? Are you writing a book?"

"Oh that part is true. I'm writing a book about a child murderer. You see, people label him as a child murderer, and they don't understand what the man is really like, what forces him to do the things that he does. He doesn't want to be a child murderer, of course he doesn't. But some of us don't want to be plumbers, though society forces us. I have invented a psychiatric detective. He saves him from himself and shows him what has happened to him. Do you understand?"

110

Douglas gazed at him piercingly with mocking eyes.

Trevor tried to put the pieces together with what was left of his mind. "So you saw him fifteen or ten years ago. You can't be more accurate than that. And you haven't seen him since. So he might be dead for all you know."

"That's about the size of it. What are you going to do now?"

The eager eyes fastened themselves on Trevor.

"Are you going to look for him?"

"What?"

"I said are you going to look for him?"

Trevor stared unseeingly ahead of him. "I don't know. I would have to get a job somewhere and stay in Australia. I don't know whether they would let me do that. I'm supposed to be going home shortly. I have my air ticket."

Douglas didn't say anything but watched him all the time. Norman might be lying dead somewhere. On the other hand he might be waiting for his brother to come and rescue him.

"One might think," he said with pedantic precision, "that there's a justice in the world which finds one out." He rose to his feet swaying.

"I should like a taxi," he said with drunken dignity.

"I'll phone for one. I don't have a phone here. I'll have to go outside," said Douglas.

"I see," said Trevor. "So that is why you didn't answer when I phoned."

It seemed to him now that he was like his brother, that like his brother he had set off to Australia not knowing where he was going, and that he had ended up confused and impotent. A bell clanged with finality in his head. "I don't know," Trevor repeated. He truly didn't know. It would all be decided for him as all this had been decided for him, that a girl called Sheila had been waiting for him, that a man called Douglas should be waiting for him here, that beneath the apparent success of his life these submarine monsters had been quietly lying in ambush. It seemed to him that he was walking unsteadily down steps into a deep, dark basement.

"I don't know," he repeated, "what I'm going to do. All I want at the moment is a taxi."

Twelve

IT OCCURRED TO him the following day that perhaps the best thing he might do was to advertise for his brother and the most convenient way of doing that was to ask for an interview on the local radio. A few weeks before, he would not have done this, for he would have considered it too public and shameful an airing of his private affairs. Nor did he know how the other lecturers and professors would react to such a naked appeal. As soon as the idea occurred to him he picked up the phone and rang the local radio station, stating what he wanted. There was a long pause and then the girl at the other end said,

"I don't see why not. We are doing a programme on the theme of exile. There are many Irish and Scots in Australia. Your appeal would fit in nicely if you linked it in some way with that theme."

"When could I do it?" Trevor asked impatiently.

"Let's see. There's actually no reason why you can't come down and record it any time. For that matter you can come this afternoon."

"I'll do that." It seemed to him that he was making a fair

demand rather than asking for a favour. He put the phone down and stared round him at the sparsely furnished room, withdrawing more and more into his surroundings, fearing that his guilt was staining them irrevocably. He went to the cupboard and poured himself a whisky. After he had finished it he had another one. Then he glanced at the sheaves of notes which he had been assembling for his lecture on Robert Louis Stevenson but they seemed irrelevant and useless. He thought again of phoning Sheila but decided against it, nor did he write a letter or a postcard. After a while he lay down on the bed and stared up at the ceiling. He was angry at Douglas for continually lying to him and deceiving him but considered also that there was an exact inevitability about how events had turned out. Douglas however shouldn't have told him that his brother was dead without overwhelming proof. Such a statement was unforgivable, but on the other hand he thought he now understood Douglas's psychology. Having been embittered by his own life, he had tried to make a more successful man than himself miserable.

He didn't have any lunch and at two o'clock in the afternoon he was in the radio station. He was met by a girl and boy: the girl was small and dark-haired, and the boy had a tentative sprouting of hair on his chin. The two apologized for their sparse knowledge of technicalities and told him that they would prefer the interview to be done in one complete block so that they wouldn't have to splice tapes. He sat in a chair between them and stared at the microphone. He had no idea what he was going to say. Normally when he did radio programmes, though in fact he hadn't taken part in many, he liked to be well prepared, but he didn't care now whether he sounded witty or inane.

There was a brief and rather rambling discussion about the

best way to handle the programme. He listened to himself taking part in the discussion but wasn't particularly interested; he was so naked and defenceless that he didn't care what anyone thought of him.

They suggested that they do a follow-up on what he had been saying about himself on the previous programme he had done with them.

"I don't mind," he said.

As the green light flashed on, the boy said, "Recently we were talking to you about your interest in Scottish literature: and we noticed that some of the interview dealt with the theme of exile. Would you like to comment further on this?"

"Yes," he said, and his mind felt extraordinarily clear and sure of itself. "At the time I was doing the interview I forgot to mention that I had a brother who came here about twenty years ago and who may be considered an exile."

"Oh?" said the girl in an interested voice.

"Yes," Trevor continued. "He left home at the age of twenty-one. I haven't seen him since. But recently I had an extraordinary experience. As a result of the last programme I did I had a phone call from a person who was at that time unknown to me and he told me that he knew my brother and had actually met him. He said he was probably an alcoholic." The word came out quite easily for he no longer cared what he admitted.

"This man told me that my brother might also have been in prison or that he might even be dead. I went to Sydney and discovered that he wasn't dead and I came back here and got in touch with this man again."

"So in fact you know very little about him," said the boy who, Trevor thought, was looking at him with a new respect because of the frank way in which he talked about his brother. "Why did he leave Britain in the first place? Why did he come to Australia?"

"It's a long complicated story. Essentially, however, it goes like this. While he was doing his National Service — I don't think you have anything like that here, though I believe you had compulsory military service at the time of Vietnam — his girl friend and myself were thrown into each other's company. When he came home we told him about it. Incidentally we are now married. He left Scotland because there was nothing much for him there. That's one reason for exile," he remarked ironically.

And then, "I suppose if I were a poet I could write a poem about it all, for that is what we do in art, explain the pain of others or our own." The girl and the boy were now looking at him with deference and excitement as if they realized they had an interesting human story on their hands. Trevor continued in the same dead, even voice, "I find now that art doesn't help in a situation like this. What I wish to do is get in touch with my brother: nothing else matters to me. The time comes when we see the inadequacy of literature."

"And you think," said the girl sympathetically, "that he is unemployed and perhaps an alcoholic?"

"I think that might be so. Almost certainly so."

"And you have no idea where he is?"

The boy looked impatiently at the girl and said, to Trevor, "How does this connect with the theme of exile? You talk about art almost contemptuously."

"Yes, I do. It's difficult to explain. What is it to be an exile? Is it not to arrive in another country and learn the language of its stones? Why is it that when you study the names of places in a new country so many of them are derived

116

from the old? It is as if the exiles arrived here and wished to surround themselves with familiar names as a child surrounds itself with toys in the night. Before the darkness comes down. Why is it that when you look at your early poets you find so many of them were alcoholics or bitter failures? Think of Lawson, for instance. Is it not the case that they were trying to build art in a rootless land? I can imagine my brother being in the same position, though he is not an artist. I must say that he is an ordinary person, no, I take that back, no person is ordinary. But I imagine him as an exile who was destroyed by this land. For all I know he may be dead somewhere. What would my job be if I were an exile? It would be to write calmly and coolly about the fact of exile. But if I were a true exile I might not be able to write at all.''

"What exactly do you mean by that?'' said the boy who was now leaning towards him.

"I mean that if you are a true exile, lost in a strange land, no art is possible, at least at the beginning. Art is the excess of comfort.'' The words sounded hollow and bitter in the small, cramped studio. "Where the heart and mind are not concerned, at their very deepest, there may be no art. It takes a long time to colonize the stones. I have been leading a privileged life since I came here.''

"So what you want to do is get in touch with him?''

"Yes, that is what I want to do.''

"But surely the circumstances you have just outlined are not the only reason for exile,'' said the boy insistently.

"No, they are not. Some, I suppose, exile themselves from a sense of adventure and a feeling of boredom. To arrive at a harmony with new surroundings is not easy. It requires that one day you see these familiar names as belonging really to the new country. One morning you wake up and find that the

117

names are not ancient phantoms at all but real places. With real people. There will be some kind of revelation.''

"Have you felt any of this yourself since you came to Australia?"

"No. I don't know. I don't think so. I want to return to the familiar darkness where I was brought up. I suppose as far as an artist is concerned he is the laureate of his own stones or nothing. For myself, I have no language for Australia.''

"But you think a language may be possible?" said the boy.

"Of course. Some day it will happen. Some day the language will spring naturally from the stones. The words will be like the dew that one sees on the flowers and leaves of one's own land. At the moment one hears the laughter from the birds but later there will be harmony."

He felt suddenly as if he was going to be sick from talking too much, and ended. "At the moment all I want is to find my brother.''

"Thank you," said the girl, but the boy was staring at him as if he had wanted him to continue, to say more about language and exile.

"That was fine," said the girl, "that will fit perfectly into our theme. It was very powerful."

"Thank you," said Trevor. "And now I'd like to go back to the college. Do you think the broadcast will help me to find him?''

"It might," said the girl.

"Good God," said Trevor suddenly. "We didn't even mention his name.''

"That's all right. We can put that in at the end. What was his name?" She sat at the desk, pen poised.

For a moment of blind terror Trevor couldn't remember

his name and then he said, "His name was Norman. Norman Grierson."

"We can add that at the end," said the girl again. "No worries."

"Thank you," said Trevor and left the studio. He walked back to the college among the colourful leaves. He thought that he must do something about his lecture on Stevenson but felt lifeless and dull. Stevenson had certainly understood and seen his own land more clearly from the perspective of exile, but his brother was not Stevenson, nor was he himself.

When he got back he drank some more whisky while at the same time trying in a desultory manner to add to his notes on Stevenson. But when he looked out of the window at the trees and the cockatoos and the pond with the leisurely gold-fish he couldn't abide where he was. He felt that he ought to move out of his sheltered room and find a more exposed one, perhaps infested with fleas. He wished to be punished by all the exiles who were weighing him down with their sadness, their gaunt open mouths. He was troubled by the ghostly sorrow of the trees, by their whiteness, by their hanging fragments of bark.

He stared down at the garden on which the darkness was falling quickly as it always did in Australia. Restlessly he left the room and walking down-town wandered about the shut shops. As he stood at a crossing he saw a parade of people with shaven heads and white cloaks walking by, ringing bells and chanting in unison. They were smiling and happy as they swayed along, as if joyful to be the centre of attraction to an admiring crowd. He felt again as if aslant to the universe. What was he doing here? What did he have in common with these shaven, chanting men whose concerns were so unimaginably different from his own?

119

He turned away and as he did so he met a boy who said to him, "Could you give me a dollar? I haven't eaten all day." For a moment it seemed to him that the boy had a Scottish accent. He put his hand in his pocket, fished out three dollars, and gave them to him. The boy thanked him profusely and then ran towards a café which was still open. After he had gone Trevor still stood there, listening to the alien chanting in the centre of the failing yellow light.

Thirteen

"I LISTENED TO your talk on the radio," said Professor
Hastie. "I thought it was a most interesting story." Trevor
looked at him in amazement: he had thought that the professor wouldn't mention the broadcast at all.

He felt light-headed, as he hadn't been sleeping very well.
He liked this professor who was more youthful than the ones
he had remembered from his own student days: indeed he
liked all the people in the department except for one female
lecturer who seemed cynical and embittered.

"That, I presume," said Hastie, "is why you asked leave
to go to Sydney?"

"Yes," said Trevor.

The professor was a boyish-looking man who had taught
originally in Cambridge and had just published a book about
Hopkins. He seemed to be the sort of man who glowed with
an easy success, and Trevor was angry when he compared
him to his brother.

"I do hope you find him," said the professor kindly.
"Please excuse me. I have a seminar."

And he glanced at his gold watch. "At eleven o'clock."

Trevor picked up his notes and made his way to the lecture room. There were perhaps ten students there and he talked to them about "Dr Jekyll and Mr Hyde" for an hour. It seemed to him that while he was talking he understood the story more clearly and that the figure of Hyde, murderous and unshaven, grew more and more sympathetic to him. When he had finished, all the students except one picked up their bags and books and left. He noticed that the one who remained behind was the one who had interviewed him on radio.

"My name's Thorn," said the student. "We talked about your brother."

"That's right," said Trevor.

"We're having a meeting tonight," said Thorn, "about Australia in general. I wondered if you would like to come along."

"Where is it being held?" said Trevor, cramming his books and notes into an attaché case that Sheila had bought for him and which could be locked by means of a code.

"It's being held in the house of a friend of mine," said Thorn. "He's unemployed. He thought you might be sympathetic."

For the first time Trevor noticed that the boy stuttered a little, perhaps from nervousness.

"What's the point of holding a meeting about society?" he said.

"That's what we do," said Thorn. "We're mostly students. We're not very experienced or organized."

"I see," said Trevor. He knew perfectly well what was happening. This boy considered that in the depths of his nature he was a protester and socialist, had sensed it to his own satisfaction.

"If you give me the address," he said, "I will be there." The boy eagerly handed him the address and departed. Trevor left the university and made his way down town. He selected a cool, dark bar, and ordered himself a whisky. Through the window he could see the bare-footed guitarist playing his energetic music.

He felt a profound change taking place in himself, as if he were a sea shifting in overwhelming freedom, and the world was tragically open to him. After he had finished his first whisky he bought another one. How perfectly mannered this city of academics and civil servants was. Professor Hastie had been so genuinely sincere and kind and yet at the same time had allowed himself to pour out a tiny, exquisite dose of friendship and sympathy and interest.

No answer had as yet come to his appeal on the radio, and he didn't really expect one. It was unlikely that Norman had ever been to Canberra, unlikely that he would be known by anyone there except Douglas, if indeed even he had known him. He passed along the arcade in a daze of confused anger. In a short while he would have to leave Australia and it appeared as if all his questions would remain unanswered. Sheila had gone to live with her mother while he was away. He didn't like her mother much and he didn't like any of her sisters. All of them would have been astounded and enraged that he had spoken so openly on the radio. But he didn't regret doing so. At last he was inspecting his life which stood like an abyss in front of him. He stared dully into his whisky glass.

When he returned to the college he lay on his bed listening to the music of the flute that wavered among the ivy-covered buildings. After a while it began to irritate him and he rose from the bed, on which he had been lying, and went in search of the musician. Eventually he found him in a room in a different block from his own. He was a young man, bearded and perplexed, who gazed apprehensively at him.

"Isn't it time you stopped practising that thing?" Trevor shouted at him. "You're getting on people's nerves."

"I'm sorry, I didn't realize. I'm sorry," said the young man.

"Well then," said Trevor and walked away, feeling that he had done something decisive and important. In the old days he would never have done what he had just done. He thought that he could howl like a wolf. He looked down at his bare arms but they were as red as ever, showing no signs of losing their rawness. But in an odd sort of way he was proud of them, as if they were a guarantee of a more real world than the one he had hitherto inhabited, medals and ribbons from a war that he had successfully waged. When he woke up, after falling asleep on the bed, it was getting dark and he washed his face and prepared to go to the meeting. The towering blocks of the city rose into the sky, with their red and green lights. He saw a plane descending toward the airfield and the moon was cold and white in the sky. He felt slightly dizzy as if from too much drink. He had to walk a long distance before he found the address which Thorn had given him. He knocked on the door and waited. At last a young man with a pony tail like a Red Indian came to the door and told him to come in.

Fourteen

"MY NAME'S HILTON. Yours?"

"Grierson. Trevor."

"I'm Harry."

"Hullo, Harry."

Harry took him into a room which looked large and unfurnished. On a table there was a big wooden bowl with salad and glasses of orange juice.

"This is Tom. Tom Grace," said Harry. "And this is Ralph Thorn. I think the two of you have met before." Trevor nodded to the young student.

The room began to fill slowly with people, mostly, as far as Trevor could see, students.

"About the salad and the orange juice," said Tom. "We club together to buy it. The speaker tonight is a man called Browning. I don't suppose you have met him?"

"No," said Trevor. "Whose place is this any way?"

"Mine and Harry's. We rent it."

"It's nice," said Trevor.

"We can't really afford to furnish it," said Tom, glancing at him enigmatically, "but it's okay. I'm not really a student. I sometimes do odd jobs but most of the time I'm unemployed.''

"And who's Browning?''

"He's a . . . he used to be a professor. He gave it all up. He's a sort of historian. Part economist as well.''

"And Harry?''

"Oh he's a student. He's doing a course in English literature. He sometimes writes short stories.''

"Are you by any chance English? Your accent.''

"Of English descent.'' Grace didn't say more but drifted away, perhaps tired of Trevor's inquisition. Hilton replaced him by Trevor's side.

"Tom's father was a colonel in the British Army you know. Tom refused to fight in Vietnam.''

"Did many do that?''

"Quite a lot. It was a brave thing to do, don't you think?''

"Yes I suppose it was for someone with that background. I don't suppose his father would have liked it. Stiff upper lip and all that.''

"He's dead now,'' said Hilton, smiling a sudden infectious smile.

A short, stocky man came over and Trevor said, "Are you a student too?''

"No,'' said the man. "I used to be a policeman. And yourself?''

"Oh I'm nothing at all,'' said Trevor abruptly. "Nothing at all.''

The other man looked at him in an odd manner but said nothing.

Eventually the speaker bustled in clutching a big, bulging attaché case. He had a small pointed beard like D. H.

Lawrence and his brow was high and white like marble. He sat down in a chair behind the table straightening some papers in front of him while Hilton introduced him in a nervous rambling fashion, at the same time making incomprehensible 'in' jokes about the university.

Trevor like the rest sat down on the floor, now and again glancing at the twenty or so serious people around him, who apart from the ex-policeman all seemed to be students.

When he met the eyes of any of them, they smiled encouragingly at him as if recognizing that he was a newcomer so that Trevor felt that he was being accepted into some kind of church. Tom Grace stood leaning against the wall in a corner by himself with an air of almost incredulous hauteur.

Browning began to speak abruptly and with some strength.

"When this country was created," he said, not referring to the large untidy mass of papers that lay before him on the table, "it was inhabited as we know by jailbirds, and aborigines. We know for instance that the father of one of our first poets, Charles Harpur, was a jailbird. Nevertheless there was a possibility that we would create a model for the future in a land of such empty spaces. This however was not done, for there was greed and rapacity and self-seeking here as elsewhere. We see, for instance, what is happening and what has happened to the aborigine. Even now prospectors are drilling among their sacred graves. The white man doesn't understand the concept of their dreamtime and doesn't try to because he himself has lost all idea of the sacred. He considers the aborigine stupid because he has never actually looked at him as a human being. But how can one call a man stupid who can survive in a boiling desert with an equipment of five basic tools? The white man who is a capitalist intent on profit has no time for such a concept as dreamtime, nor inclination to read the aborigine's legends which are beautiful and complex with the beauty and complexity of poetry. He cannot understand that there is a relationship with nature other than exploitation. Consequently he uses towards the aborigine a mixture of threat and patronage. It never occurs to him that his own inner emptiness is anything other than superiority nor that other ways of seeing the world are possible. He thinks that if the aborigine is given a few gifts equivalent to glass beads he should be grateful and not bother him again. Not so long ago I read in one of our newspapers a story of an owner of a pub throwing flour over an aborigine to see what he would look like as a white man.

"It was, as I have said, possible to create in this country a model of a classless society but that opportunity has been thrown away. We have a Prime Minister who, himself rich, does not understand the problems of the poor. He is arrogant and unsympathetic. Why do we have in this potentially rich land of ours such a high rate of unemployment? Why is unemployment pay so low? How is it that we are now seeing the Great Barrier Reef itself being threatened by prospectors and drillers? Is it not the case that the man who is admired nowadays is the unscrupulous exploiter and in short the capitalist? Is this what our early poets looked forward to?

"Australia was founded by unwilling exiles but a lot of people are exiles within this potentially rich land. If you look at Canberra itself you will see clearly enough who its real inhabitants are. It is civil servants, government employees obsessed with their respective grades. And what is the first question they ask each other when they are introduced at parties. It is the question: 'What scale are you on? How much are you earning?' " He looked around him aggressively and then said,

"Isn't that the case?

"This, as you know, is an artificial city. It doesn't even have the rough reality of Sydney.

"How is it that we have allowed a beautiful country to become what she now is, a country of classes, just like the eternal motherland, though the classes here are perhaps not so obvious as they are in Britain, since I don't suppose we have for instance the differentiation of accents that they have there? But is it not the case that Fraser is an admirer of Mrs Thatcher and probably keeps a picture of her above his bed, or under it as far as I know?

"And what sort of Labour Party do we have? Is it a real revolutionary party? I feel guilty when I see our so-called top classes, our bureaucrats and academics drinking their wine, holding their lavish conferences, protecting themselves against economic storms. Is it not high time that Australia became Australia and fulfilled her own destiny? Is it not high time that it ceased to mourn its dying motherland, that its inhabitants ceased to think of themselves as exiles, that they took on the burden of being themselves in a real world? I was talking yesterday to a man who told me that he couldn't afford to have medical attention because of the high prices. Who are the people with the highest salaries in our country? Precisely, the doctors. We fought in Vietnam while at the same time we had the scandal of the aborigine in our midst, our flagrant paternalism. I know of many graduates from our universities who cannot get employment. But at the same time I have been at parties where I have encountered ambassadors from other countries and we have talked amiably about the events of the world as if these events did not cast a shadow

129

on ourselves. How can we live like this when the producers of our real wealth are underpaid?

"We should be a country of high idealism and yet what are we? We are the slavish lackeys of the United States, trying to stop athletes going to the Olympics while business firms are still trading with Russia, debating whether we should stop exports to Iran and wondering at the same time whether our principles will not cost us too much money.

"And what have we to look forward to but years and years of this government after the scandal of Whitlam was perpetrated? We all know that he didn't lose his premiership for doing too little but for trying to do too much. And if any of you attend parliament what do you see there? Orderlies who tell you to be silent while the proceedings are conducted in an undignified uproar. Members of Parliament have been known to call each other 'fat pigs' and ask each other 'to come outside'.

In this land of infinite potential riches why should so many families be living on the borderline while inflation rises and prices accelerate? Is that what our fathers had in mind when they held in their minds an idealistic vision of Australia? I myself left my professorship because more and more I saw I was living in an unreal circle of privilege, when I saw that my historical monographs were decorative scribblings on a void. It is this which sticks in my throat and refuses to be swallowed. It is time that we spoke out, that we stood in front of Parliament House with our placards and said what we believed in and said it publicly."

Amid cheering Browning sat down looking around him with an aggressive stare as if he believed that his audience was the enemy. After he had finished the ex-policeman stood up and said, "I agree with what the professor has said. I say that

130

the policeman is the servant of the upper classes and always has been. Do you think a Senator will be treated in the same way as a member of the lower classes? Of course one doesn't find this only in Australia, one finds it everywhere, but as the Professor said we expected more of this country. I have been a policeman in New Guinea and when a native policeman gets his salary there all his unemployed relatives gather round him and he gives them so much of it every week. Why should you do that, I asked him. They expect it, he said. It was because of their tribalism they expected this. It was because of their sense of community. Of course in a way it is unfair but it shows that the ones in work are expected to be responsible for the ones who aren't. If we don't have responsibility for each other what have we?''

A young student at the back stood up and began to speak in a quick nervous voice. ''My name's Hilary Chase,'' he said, ''and I know perfectly well and every other student here knows perfectly well that all we do at our universities is try to gain good grades. Our examination system is a travesty of education. How is it that we find ourselves competing with each other for certificates when so many people in the world are starving? How can we sit and listen to boring lectures day after day when we know that terrible events are happening in the real world? We are a sausage factory and that is a fact. Professor Browning talked of idealism but where is the idealism in the education system? Is it just for gaining grades that we go to a university?''

And so the discussion went on. Trevor felt around him the resentment of those who sensed obscurely that society was ranked against them and at the centre of it he saw his own brother curled up like a tramp in a ditch, asking for work on a sheep farm, sleeping in a seedy room. He too felt that this country, vast and new, could have been an example to the world but that something had gone wrong, that the corruption which was to be found in secretive Europe, in brash America, was to be found here as well. It seemed to him that what Browning had said was true, that the world in which he himself lived was a rich, privileged world, that he had never considered that other world which like a dark, invisible star accompanied the golden, glowing one till by its gravity it pulled one into it.

As he listened to the professor and the students preparing to hold their protest outside Parliament House the following day he remembered seeing Fraser sitting on a bench in Parliament, leaning forward arrogantly towards a scurrying minion, turning away from the Opposition benches, languorously standing up and making a short speech, secure in the knowledge of power.

Browning and Grace came over to speak to him while Thorn and Hilton hovered on the periphery.

"I liked your speech," said Trevor to the professor.

"Thank you," said Browning, looking modest and easy in his success. "I believe you are at the university."

"For a short while."

"And you're from Scotland."

"That's right."

"I was reading something about the Clearances recently. By a man called Prebble. Do you know him?"

"I haven't met him."

"And another book by a man called Grimble. He said that Harriet Beecher Stowe approved of the Clearances, some of which took place, I believe, in Sutherland."

"That is the ironical thing," said Trevor. "She did. She couldn't see that a similar thing to what happened with the

132

negroes was happening in Scotland."

"I understand," said Browning, sipping an orange juice. "We all live in contexts. Some of our Australian writers have strong social consciences. You must meet them."

He added, "You have met Tom here. He is one of our heroes. He refused, quite rightly, to fight in the Vietnam War."

'I had heard of that," said Trevor.

"Yes, he defied his lares and penates. Not everyone has the courage to do that." Trevor felt uncomfortable with Browning as if he were talking to someone who understood him. In the past he had attended so many parties where people spoke briefly to each other, though they had nothing to say, skidded words like stones across ice, glanced over each other's shoulders as if they were awaiting the ultimately brilliant and witty remark that never came, talked about their progeny, had an air of invincible rightness as if the world belonged to them. He remembered talking to a Swedish sociologist who had said to him, "The Australians don't like touching each other. Yet they always call you by your first name when they meet you."

"Tell me," he said, "do Australians look back to their past?"

"Some of them," said Browning. "The Irish especially. Some of them consider this to be a new house which doesn't have the creaking sounds of the old one, and this makes them feel uncomfortable. They long for the noises of a real past. On the other hand, this is now a multi-racial society, which turns as easily to the East as to the West."

Quite without thinking Trevor said to Hilton and Grace, "I wonder if it would be possible for me to stay here tonight. I don't want to go back to the college."

"Sure," they said as if they understood what he was trying to say. "You're taking part in the demonstration tomorrow?"

"Of course I am."

A cluster of students had gathered round Browning, whom they admired greatly for resigning from his post and Grace said, "He threw up his job as a professor. As a matter of fact he was getting bad reviews in scholarly journals for his history books which were considered too political. He writes for magazines and newspapers now."

"What does he write?"

"He writes quite a lot about Ned Kelly. He considers him a social critic."

When the others apart from Hilton and Grace had gone Trevor said to the latter, "Tell me what happened in connection with the Vietnam War."

"There's nothing to tell. I was in jail for a while."

"It was a brave thing," said Trevor. "I would have done National Service if I had been called up, though I know of some who protested. And some COs. from the last war. Aggression is a strange thing."

"What do you mean?" said Grace.

"Just that this CO I know — Conscientious Objector — is intellectually very aggressive and sometimes cruel while on the other hand he would not be so, physically. And then of course there is the phenomenon of Tolstoy and Gandhi — the outward peace, the inner turmoil."

"Of course," said Grace, and then, "You think this aggression is natural to man?"

"Sometimes I think that, sometimes not. By the way did you do this?" he asked pointing to a model of a sailing ship.

"Yes. I work on them when I have spare time, which I

134

have quite a lot of," he said almost bitterly.

"And what do you do in your spare time, Harry?"

"Oh, I study astrology."

"I beg your pardon?"

"Astrology. It's a fascinating subject."

Grace took out a bottle of wine and they drank it. During the course of the evening Trevor was shown more models of sailing ships with their sails set, as if in fact they were setting out for Australia, though they were fixed calmly inside bottles. He went to bed in a rather bare room in which there was a large star map. He slept soundly for the first time since he had heard about his brother. In the dark room a white ship lay motionless under the artificial stars.

Fifteen

THE TWENTY OR so of them stood outside Parliament House carrying their banners and and slogans which said THE POOR HAVE A RIGHT TO WORK and COULD YOU LIVE ON UNEMPLOYMENT PAY, FRASER? Trevor stood among them holding up his own banner. The Parliament buildings were white in the sun and not far away he could see a park where fountains changed shape continually, creating momentary sculptured effects. Two policemen stood outside the door on the steps above, gazing down at them. The atmosphere was friendly and companionable and Trevor felt much as he had done many years before when he had clinked his can for charity in his university days in Glasgow.

"Remember, this is a peaceful demonstration," said Browning, who was clad in shirt sleeves and shorts as if he were on holiday.

"FRASER OUT, FRASER OUT," the students begans to shout.

A bus made its way slowly past and a crowd of school-children in green uniforms got out with their teachers. They crossed the street and climbed the steps. Then the street was empty again.

"They're being shown our parliament at work," said Grace wryly.

The two policemen stood quietly watching them.

The rhythm seemed suddenly to grow faster.

"FRASER OUT, FRASER OUT."

"FRASER OUT," Trevor heard himself shouting.

One of the policemen moved over to them. "Keep on the sidewalk," he said. "Move back from the street."

They all moved back, still chanting.

Trevor found himself staring with enmity at the policeman who was dressed in a blue shirt, his sleeves rolled up, while at his side there was a holster with a gun in it. It was as if his mind suddenly became confused and he really thought that his brother had died in a police station, though it was now clear that he hadn't. Nevertheless it seemed to him that the policeman was his fated opponent, as if it was he who had compelled him to be where he was.

What on earth was the meaning of this demonstration? How could one change a society by standing on a pavement on a fine morning such as this? He swayed as if in a heavy wind. One voice said, "More than this will have to be done." The other said, "You're a stranger in this country. What is all this to you?" A car suddenly appeared and a shout went up, "Here's Fraser. Here's Fraser." The twenty students swept forward with their banners and the chant became even louder and almost primitive in its intensity.

"FRASER OUT, FRASER OUT." The car swung in a curve towards the steps.

They saw Fraser getting out, accompanied by two broad-shouldered men who looked like bodyguards. He ran up the steps and as he did so the twenty of them crossed the road still

137

shouting. Somehow in the rush Trevor saw that the policeman was lying on the ground, his face looking up at him. I
cannot hurt him, he thought, though I could. I could quite
easily do so at this moment, but I won't. And he heard
himself shouting, "Move back, move away from him."

The world had become a blur and there was a continual
swirling and shoving. Policemen were running down the
steps and Fraser and his bodyguards had disappeared.

"Come on," said Grace, "get the hell out of here. My
car is over there." Trevor began to run and while he was
running he was thinking of the policeman. "He is a human
being," he thought. "I cannot harm him. How could I
kick him while he was lying on the ground?" And yet at
the same time he thought of his own brother being kicked,
he saw him with blood on his face, his long coat hanging
down to his feet, as if he were a figure from Dickens.

And even while he was running he despised himself,
"How can the world be changed if there is no hurt?" He
looked back and saw that there were still some people wres-
tling with the police and that everywhere there were banners, some raised and moving, others lying on the ground.
He saw that Browning was struggling in the arms of a
policeman.

"I'll have to go back," he shouted to Grace.

"Don't be a bloody idiot," Grace shouted back at him.
Trevor saw others running to their cars as well and was
slightly comforted.

"Get the hell into the car," said Grace to him. "What
do you think you'd achieve? They'd ruin you."

"I ca . . ." He tried to speak but the words wouldn't
come out. He saw a policeman running along the road and
turned and threw a stone at him.

"What the hell do you think you're doing?" said Grace. "Get in the car."

He found himself in the car and Grace was driving recklessly out of the street they were on, accelerating, turning corners. After a while they had left the demonstration behind them and were driving more slowly.

"I should have stayed," he almost wept. "But I couldn't . . ."

"Couldn't have what?" said Grace impatiently, his eye on the mirror.

"I couldn't hurt him. He was lying there on the ground. And I couldn't hurt him." And then he thought, "If they had caught me, they would have kept me behind, and I wouldn't have been able to look for my brother."

"We can't use violence," said Grace. "How can we?"

Trevor knew that Grace had saved him and was grateful.

"Thanks," he said to him.

"No worries," said Grace, manoeuvring the car past a large truck that suddenly loomed out of the fresh, clear morning.

"That's not the way to do it," said Grace. "I told Browning that. It won't get us anywhere. It's child's play. We have to organize better than this."

"How can we do it then?" said Trevor.

"We have to get the unions behind us. We're just amateurs."

"It's a start," said Trevor.

"What sort of start? And what can students do? It's laughable."

"What will happen to these people if they are arrested?" said Trevor.

"Oh they might be fined. Or they might just be warned."

"And Browning?"

"Probably the same. I don't know."

"And we ran away."

"There was nothing we could do. What was the point of getting ourselves arrested?"

"We could have stayed and spoken out."

"And what would that have done for us?" said Grace. "Nothing. We're amateurs. We're not serious."

And his face grew grim.

"What will they think of us now?" said Trevor. "The ones who have been arrested. Will they speak to us again?"

"That's not the point. The point is that we got away. They have nothing on us. It was a childish escapade anyway."

"Is that what you think?"

"Of course. Haven't I told you? I just know it was right to retire in good order." And for a moment it was as if Trevor heard Grace's military father speaking through him.

At the same time he sensed that Grace had qualities of leadership which Browning didn't have. He was a man who was willing to see a campaign in terms not just of tactics but of strategy. He remembered him leaning almost contemptuously against the wall the previous night while listening to Browning.

"You mean," he said, "that you are thinking of starting something yourself?"

"I mean that Browning is a fool. In any case he has the wrong motives."

"Wrong motives?"

"He's disaffected for the wrong reasons. There's more to a campaign like this than people's vanities. We are at a moment of decision in Australia. Do we want to follow

America, dig uranium? We are a people on our own. We have a right to choose.''

They drew up outside Grace's house. ''But what if other people won't let you make your own decisions?'' said Trevor as they left the car and went inside.

''They will have to. Why should we be prevented from holding the Olympics, for example? We are doing what America tells us. Browning was right to this extent that we have thrown away a huge opportunity to be ourselves, to choose our own destiny. Want an orange juice?''

''Yes, please,'' said Trevor who felt inordinately thirsty after his running.

''How long have you got here?'' said Grace.

''Not long. Just about a week.'' In a strange way he thought that by leaving Australia he would be leaving his home. This huge land, brown and withered with drought, seemed to have suddenly become the truth teller, a dusty oracle which might tell him about himself.

''There is nothing that can be done in this way,'' said Grace, sipping his orange juice. ''I'm English but I love Australia. I don't know whether you've noticed it but there's a depth and mystery to this country that attracts one like a secret bride. Have you ever seen any of Boyd's paintings?''

''Yes,'' said Trevor.

''I think he's better than Nolan, more mysterious,'' said Grace. ''It seems to me that this is a sensitive land and someone must listen to its voice. Our leaders have converted it into a country just like any other country, when it's so obviously different from most.''

''But what will you do?'' said Trevor.

''I shall go into politics,'' said Grace simply. ''There must be enough people who think like me.''

141

"But can you go into politics just like that?"

"I shall have to come out and speak. If there is truth in me I will be heard. We are not talking about evil men. We are talking about men without vision. I shall say the same thing over and over till someone will hear me. We had the chance of making this a great country and we have failed. I don't believe in violence. People are bound to listen at last if I speak the truth. Listen," he said urgently. "When I lie in my bed at night I hear a voice which tells me: This is a new land, this is a different country. You cannot let it become like any other. In England I felt that the country has said all that it has to say, and that its voice is now full of contradictions. But here the contradictions aren't as yet everywhere. This land hasn't reached the state where its voice can no longer be heard. I will simply present myself as a man who has something to say and if my voice has conviction it will be heard. I believe that. The vision itself will speak. Listen: this place is as yet young. It has hardly even been populated. We still have the chance of going the way we have to go. And it isn't Fraser's way. We have to learn to be what we truly are in the depths of ourselves. We have to take the responsibility for ourselves. In the depths of our consciousness we are at the moment colonials but we must learn to step out into the real world."

"Yes," said Trevor. "That is what you must do."

"It is not the consciousness of students we need," said Grace. "It is the consciousness of those who have suffered and who have seen the same vision as I have. There are a few of them. They understand that there are things which belong to the past and things which belong to the future. We must learn to have the courage of being new.

"Come in," he said, and Trevor turned and found himself looking at Douglas who was smiling as he entered.

142

Sixteen

"MALCOLM AND I were in university together," said Tom Grace, looking from one to the other.

"I dropped out though," said Douglas.

"Malcolm is one of my most valuable friends," said Grace, "he's been to places that I've never been to."

"And that book you're writing," said Trevor casually. "How are you getting on with it?"

"Oh fine, fine. You see, Tom, when I met Trevor first," said Douglas with slight bitterness, "he didn't think I could possibly have had a university education. He attached a label to me, I was a drop-out. Alcoholic." Trevor gazed at the star globe which sat on top of the television set: he had been more surprised than he could tell by seeing Douglas there. It seemed to him that the globe was rotating slowly and that destinies were in some way fashioned by the stars. "I did something unforgivable," said Douglas. "I allowed my personal feelings to take control of me. I heard this self-sufficient voice, so literary and plump, going on about exile, and I thought 'This man doesn't know anything about life.' "

"And you told me a lot of lies," said Trevor furiously, not

caring whether Grace had been told the story or not.

"I wanted to see what you would do, whether you had any feelings. I know where your brother is. I found out quite by chance."

"What?"

"I really do."

"Where is he then?"

"I'll take you to him."

"When?"

"Tomorrow if you like."

"Why didn't you do that before?"

"You should know the answer to that."

"I suppose you studied psychology in the university?"

"That among other things." He passed his hand across his forehead as if he had another headache.

"The bit about my headaches is true." He turned to Grace and said, "So it was all a washout."

"Yes, mate," said Grace ironically, and Trevor found it difficult to adjust his view of Douglas as someone who knew both Grace and him, as someone who lived in a real society. This was in fact a man who was more knowledgeable than himself, who had dived into the deep, mysterious underworld of Sydney for his own reasons.

"My father," said Douglas, "couldn't get a job here, when he came. Remember I told you he had come over from Scotland. He had no money for a while and later he left us. I couldn't afford to stay in university. Then both my father and mother died and I drifted. But all the time I was taking notes, watching. Tom and I have always been idealists," he added ironically.

"And Thorn and Hilton, what about them?" said Trevor to Grace.

144

Grace shrugged his shoulders. "They won't bother with them. Why should they? But we'll maybe have to see Simmons," he said to Douglas.

"Yes," said Douglas and turning to Trevor said, "What I told you in other respects is true. I've seen knife fights. I've seen a great number of drifters of this world, people at the very limit of their resources. And I don't like seeing it, there must be a way of avoiding that. Your brother just about survived but you wouldn't have, though you're not as priggish as you were."

"Thanks," said Trevor and Grace intervened.

"Has Murray arrived?" he asked Douglas.

"Tomorrow. I think he's flying down."

"Right. I'll meet him."

Suddenly he turned to Trevor and said, "Have I shown you my model of the sailing ship?"

"Beautiful," said Douglas. "Isn't she? Sails and everything. A real beaut."

"That's what I've spent a lot of my time on," said Grace proudly, adding, "But did you ever know anything about the lives people led on board these ships? It's like the ones that brought the first jailbirds to Australia." He added, "It's the mining of course that destroyed the country and created the greed. Browning's book about that aspect isn't good, it's not scholarly enough, he's a romantic you see. The big capitalists moved in with their machinery and the small man couldn't compete. But she's beautiful, isn't she?"

They gazed at the ship for a long time, as she lay motionless with sails set in the rather sultry room.

As if continuing an earlier conversation Douglas said, "I was with Tom here in university. As I told you my people came from Ayrshire. They saw enough capitalism there."

145

His face darkened. "I'm interested in the psychology of capitalism. Did you know that for a long time in Germany mining boards could prevent you from marrying till you were twenty-four? Miners were a kind of slaves at one time. I lived with some aborigines for a while."

"And where did you actually meet my brother?"

"In Sydney as I told you. I had a feeling that you would go and see the Salvation Army but they have their own reasons for helping. They remain within the system. They have a plate of soup in one hand but a Bible in the other."

"The woman was very kind," said Trevor defensively.

"Naturally. And why not? But do they really understand people like your brother? Of course not. You don't understand him yourself. And yet you are his brother."

"I don't seem to understand anything," said Trevor helplessly.

"But you're learning, you're learning."

"We're setting off early tomorrow," Douglas added.

"Are we taking the bus?"

"Naturally. I can't afford the plane."

"In that case I insist on paying," said Trevor fiercely.

"There you go again. Will you never understand that a man has his pride? I said I would take you to see your brother because I like him. I'll pay my own fare. He was a mate of mine." He was suddenly offended again and it was as if Trevor saw prickles rising on him like a thistle.

He felt continually, in his presence, as though he were walking through a minefield.

"Can you set up the meeting then?" said Grace.

"With Murray you mean. Saturday morning would be the best. By that time I'll be back from Sydney."

"Good."

Douglas turned to Trevor and asked, "Have you anything to do today then?"

"Not today. Tomorrow I'll see you at the bus station at ten."

"Right."

There was a silence and Trevor said uneasily, "I'd better go to the bank then."

No one spoke and he added, "I'll need some money for Sydney."

"If you'll excuse me," he ended lamely, "I'd better go now." He left the house and began to walk to the Civic Centre. It seemed to him that his head was spinning and that he was attacked as if by culture shock. Now and again he would glance in a shop window and remember Sheila who if she had been with him would have been stopping now and again to admire rings and bracelets. She seemed very distant from him at that moment. He had been enchanted by this brown, droughty land: in the centre of it there was a dumb music that he wished to hear. The long-haired guitar player was still there while at his feet was a cap with a few coins in it. He went over and put a dollar in the cap but the guitar player didn't stop playing and didn't look at him. He had a thirst to go to the library but didn't do so. He sat down on a bench and stared down at the ground. It seemed to him that it was himself and not his brother who was wandering in this country. What was he doing? Could he go back and live with Sheila as if nothing had happened? He passed his hand across his brow as Douglas was in the habit of doing. How innocent he was, an innocent abroad, while all around him were the complexities of a real developing land. How every word that he spoke to Douglas seemed to be the wrong one.

What would he say to his brother when he eventually met

him? How would the latter forgive him for what he had done to him? He remembered again the wedding and the exhibition Norman had made of himself, shouting loudly and buying drinks for everybody and then at the end coming up to him and shaking him by the hand, he who had felt so much like a Judas. "It's all right, it's all right," Norman had kept saying over and over, swaying slightly. And then three weeks afterwards he had left on the ship. He recalled with a gush of warmth how the two of them had used to play football together, and sometimes even cricket with hand-made stumps: but that had been a long time ago. And a picture of the leafy wood returned to him on that particular summer's day when he had run through the trees hiding from Norman, the shadows dappling the glades. His brother had shouted his name over and over. But he himself had hidden behind a tree and Norman's voice had at last faded into the distance.

"You've had everything, and I've had nothing," he seemed to hear his brother shouting and Trevor saw a picture of himself as if dressed in a peasant's hat, shaped like a dome of an Eastern temple, while he bent down in a field, digging.

How easily the mind could disguise reality from itself. With what adamant blindness he had walked through the world not seeing himself as he really was. Astonished, he raised his head and looked at the sky where a double-barrelled trail left by a jet plane still lingered fuzzily. He could not see the plane at all though he could see the parallel twin tracks. He and his brother were running across a hot field, their shadows alongside each other, Norman's face was freckled and tanned, and his teeth were white and small. The track they left was ghostly and undefined.

Soon he would have to leave the country and it was as if he

was leaving a part of himself behind. He suddenly got up and entered a newspaper shop that was at the end of the arcade. Among the Australiana he found a book of poems translated from an aboriginal language. He read quickly.

With its keen eyes the gull saw the small tracks of
    the mice,
mouse tracks leading into the grass and the foliage.
The gull circles around flapping its wings and crying,
It is always there at the wide expanse of water, at the
    place of the Sacred Tree, diving down, probing
    about with its beak.
The sound of its flapping wings, as it swoops down
    on a mouse . . .
It is always there, that bird among the western people,
    its cry spreading over the country during the wet
    season, the time of the new grass . . .
and the squeaking cry of the mouse.
It is mine, says the gull, I spear the mouse on its track,
    holding it in my beak
the squeak of the mouse and the cry of the gull
    echoing up to the sky . . .

It seemed to him as he read that he could recognize the images and that they were like pictures of home and that across whatever seas divided him from Scotland this poetry came to him as fresh as if it had been written in his own country.

Seventeen

ON THE BUS the following day Douglas was at first moodily silent while Trevor didn't know exactly how he himself felt. He was partly excited and partly afraid.

"How is your book going?" he asked Douglas at last.

"Fine. I'm almost finished. Another four weeks should do it." Trevor thought he looked ill and indeed Douglas himself went on to say, "I feel claustrophobic on these buses. I feel as if I could smash the panes. Maybe I shouldn't have been as brutal as I was with you, when I phoned and told you your brother was dead. I had a bad headache at the time."

"That's all right," said Trevor." I suppose I had it coming to me."

"I couldn't stand the university," Douglas continued. "One day I just packed it in. Then for years and years I had no money. It was a bad time: I used to sleep in parks. You've never done that, have you? I once fought in a pub with a man who was nearly mad, and who almost killed me. I suppose you think I'm a compulsive liar. Your brother actually doesn't read books, I don't know why I said that. He could have gone to university if he had wanted to. What will you do when you get back to Scotland?''

"I don't know. I suppose I shall carry on lecturing.''

"I think truth is good for people,'' said Douglas abruptly.
"I don't think people should live in an illusion. That man
Browning you were speaking to doesn't understand anything. Not even my friend Tom does. They both have a
literary consciousness. Neither of them has wakened up in
the morning and not realized where his next meal was coming from. Have you ever read anything by Lawson? His
hoboes set off into the blue humping their bluey. Do you
know why I left the university? One day I looked at a
question paper — I was doing English as well as Psychology
— and it said, 'Comment on Hardy's use of archaic language
in his poems.' I looked and looked at that question and it
came to me quite clearly that it had nothing to do with
anything, even with Thomas Hardy. I walked out of the
examination room and got drunk. I don't suppose you've
ever done anything like that?''

"Not like that,'' said Trevor. "How do you think my
brother will react when he sees me?''

"I don't know. What if it isn't your brother I'm taking
you to at all? What if it is someone else? What if I knock you
out as that fellow did in Sydney? Have you thought of that?''
And his eyes glittered dangerously. "Don't you realize the
power I exert over you? You're dependent on me.''

Trevor, who didn't know what to say since he had actually thought these things, was silent. It seemed to him that
Douglas was on the verge of madness, that he was entirely
unpredictable.

Douglas became moody again, staring out at the monotonous landscape.

"I don't care about your brother. He was just a mate. We

were ships that passed in the night. Deep down you don't care much about him either. You are going to meet him out of a sense of duty. We are all liars and hypocrites.''

He paused and then added, contemptuously,

"You want to come out here and save your brother. It gives you a sense of superiority. But what if he doesn't want to be saved? He stole food from me once, did I ever tell you that?''

"No, you didn't.''

"We had a fight. I can't remember who won. Yes, I do, I won. But the following morning we were mates again. Remember that child murderer I talked to you about. He didn't want to be a child murderer. But it is very easy to pick up a paper and say, "Oh a child murderer,'' and leave it at that. He was in fact a man of over sixty with a low IQ. He was unshaven, he had a big nose and black teeth: he was human. When he was asked in court why he had killed these children he said he didn't know. You shouldn't go and see your brother at all. You should go home. People are so stupid. Go home, there's nothing for you here.''

Trevor was about to point out to him that it was he himself who had started him on this chase but he didn't say anything as he didn't want to irritate him.

"You see,'' said Douglas, "I was actually a psychiatric nurse for a while and Norman was brought in to dry out. He had a hard time of it. He should have married.'' And he looked closely at Trevor. "So should I. But then if you marry you enter another system. I wish to hell this bus would hurry up. I used to listen to your brother at night. He became delirious, you know. He would talk about you and your mother and about his girl friend. One day I mentioned this to him and he punched me. He had to be restrained. How do

152

you think he will like it when you take him home and he is so clearly a failure. Have you considered that? Is he not going to be envious of you? Did you know that I write poetry as well as prose?''

"Oh?" said Trevor, politely.

"There you go again. You immediately think my poetry is no good. It probably isn't but that isn't the point. Why did you automatically think my poetry is no good? Because you have never heard of me before. And because you think that my personality is not the sort you associate with poetry. You don't really want to talk to me but you're too gentlemanly to say so.'' He suddenly sat up in his seat as if a new thought had occurred to him. "What's so special about your brother anyway? Have you ever thought of helping me? No, of course not. Not that I need your help. I don't want a damn thing from you. You are saying to yourself, 'I wish I had never got myself into this box.' Aren't you? Tell me the truth. You're not a gentleman, you're a coward. You're like Grace and Browning, you're all poseurs. Do you think any of you are going to change the world? Of course not.'' Trevor had the most intense desire to sleep. He felt as if he were under continual siege by an enemy on whom at the same time he depended, that his personality was cracking under this ceaseless tirade.

"Don't you like my brother?'' he said at last.

"Well, it's like this. His personality isn't developed, he is at a low level of consciousness. Why did he run away to Australia? Have you ever thought of that? I bet he told you before he left that he didn't want to stand in your way. I would have hit you if I had been in his place. Tell me the truth. Was he the chivalrous gentleman?''

"He did say that he didn't want to stand in my way,'' said Trevor.

"So he walked out into the snow, like Oates. Or perhaps he didn't wish to marry that girl after all. Couldn't he have done so before he had joined the Army? Perhaps he was jealous of you and couldn't stand you being in his light. Do you think he gave you his real reason for coming to Australia? What exactly did he say to you before he left?"

"Nothing much. He got drunk the previous night and said he hoped the two of us would be happy."

"He should have punched you on the nose. You pity your brother. Perhaps he doesn't need your pity. You're staring at me all the time, did you know, as if I was Mephistopheles. And you were Faust or someone. Or perhaps even Gretchen. Tell me, do you think there is something devilish about me? I'm sure you do. You feel happier when you can make me literary, a demon from a book. But I'm not a character in a book you know, I'm a real person." And his eyes glittered feverishly. "And a lot of the time I can't stand you. What Grace and Browning and people like you forget is what people are really like, real people. They don't themselves belong to the lower classes and so they think the lower classes are essentially decent, likeable, friendly. Well, some are and some are not. They're infected like everyone else. I belong to the lower classes and I'm infected. I wonder why you ran away from that demonstration. You were frightened, weren't you? Isn't that right? When are you ever going to see yourself as you really are, superfluous and hollow?" His face looked suddenly drawn and white and Trevor thought that perhaps he was ill, that perhaps he didn't eat, and hadn't had any breakfast. But he didn't wish to offer him food when the bus stopped at the restaurant it had stopped at the last time: he had already made the mistake of offering to pay his fare.

154

"Why can't you come straight out and say that you hated your brother and your brother hated you?" said Douglas. "There's nothing unusual about that, it's not even unnatural in my opinion. Did you know that most murders take place within families? Why don't you just follow your instincts and have nothing to do with me or your brother? Why don't you just ignore me? You know," he said, "that your brother attacked me one night in hospital. He thought I was you." He glanced at Trevor with the same mocking, saturnine smile. "It's true, you know. He got me by the throat. 'Bastard' he was shouting. He nearly killed me. Well, have you nothing to say about that?"

"I'm listening," said Trevor. "You're probably telling me the truth."

"Of course I'm telling you the truth," said Douglas angrily. "I told you that the Pole was a compulsive liar though. Maybe I am too. Only I say the lies out loud, you just think them. If you love your wife go home to her. Forget about Norman. I'm telling you, just go home. I'll be leaving you with him. I have to go back to Canberra."

"I have to see him," said Trevor. "I won't go back."

"What if he's ill and delirious? What if he comes at you with a knife?"

"I have to see him," Trevor repeated dully. "Anyway when I get back I might leave the university. Sheila won't like it but I may have to do it."

"Perhaps she was a prize you wished to take from your brother?"

"No," Trevor shouted and then more calmly after glancing at the rest of the passengers in the bus. "That's not true. That's a lie."

155

"Think about it," said Douglas. "Just think about it. I've been sent here to be your devil's advocate. Maybe I don't exist. You couldn't stay in Australia, I doubt if you could get a job here. How old are you?"

"Forty-one," said Trevor.

"Well then you're too old. You can't stay here. You'll have to go back."

"Yes," said Trevor. "I'll have to go back. Some day you may come over to Scotland and see me."

"Not a chance," said Douglas. "I don't like you all that much and anyway I don't have any money."

He shut his eyes and then opened them restlessly a few minutes later.

"Have you ever thought that I am your shadow, your other self, your *doppelgänger*?" he asked, his eyes shining. "I travel beside you and I speak the truth to you. I may be your Hyde which you hide."

"You're a friend of Grace's," said Trevor in a sudden panic. "He knows you."

Hyde, hide, hide, said the voice in the wood as they travelled on. The Black Douglas.

> Last night I dreamed a dreary dream
> beyond the Isle of Skye
> I dreamt a dead man won a fight
> and that dead man was I. . . .

He shuddered and stared straight ahead of him. Douglas was moving his head restlessly against the back of the seat as if he were suffering a dreadful nightmare. The bus raced on through the blue perspex landscape.

156

Eighteen

WHEN THEY ARRIVED at the bus station Douglas said, "I don't want to do any more travelling. I'll have to go and room with a friend of mine. you'll have to go and see your brother on your own."

"What do you mean?" said Trevor.

"What I just said. You'll have to go and see him on your own. I feel sick. I've got a bad headache."

"You can't do that," shouted Trevor.

"Why can't I? I'll give you the address."

"You may give me the wrong address."

"Are you calling me a liar?" said Douglas angrily.

"I'm just saying that I'm not going to be pushed around by you any more. You promised you would take me to him."

"I didn't promise anything of the kind." Out of the corner of his eye Trevor saw a big bus entering the bus station and looming towards him; he stepped aside.

"I'm fed up with being pushed around," he said. "First of all you phone me out of the blue and tell me a lie and now you don't want to come with me." He was almost inarticulate with anger, and it seemed to him at that moment that he was seeing Douglas for the first time. The eyes, he noticed, were almost jet black, as was the hair, and the cheeks were hollow.

"I'm fed up with it," he shouted.

"What if you find your brother is a homosexual?" said Douglas mockingly. "What if he's living with another man? Morton told you that."

"Morton was a liar," Trevor shouted.

"You never know. Your brother might have been in that house. Why do you think he never married that girl?"

"Look," said Trevor, "if you say that again I'll . . ."

"You'll what?"

"I'll bloody well punch you. I'll fight you. I'm tired of all this."

Suddenly Douglas smiled at him, an open, winning, boyish smile, and said in a quiet voice, "It's okay. Here's the address. This time I'm telling you the truth. I found it out quite by chance. I've got it written down here." And he took a piece of paper from his wallet.

"You're not a bad lad really. Take it."

Trevor looked suspiciously at the paper as if it might explode in his face.

"Are you sure this is the right one at last?" he asked urgently.

"Yes, I'm sure," said Douglas in the same quiet voice. "This is where he is staying. and now I'll have to go."

"Are you sure you have to go? Can't you come with me?"

"I don't think you need me any more," said Douglas in a low voice. "Look after yourself. But you'll be all right." And he turned away.

"Look," said Trevor, "I know it's not my business. But won't you take some money? I don't believe you're staying with a friend."

Douglas stood and looked at him for a long time and then said, "all right then. If you've got ten dollars. I won't take any more. And I have a friend to stay with. Don't worry."

"Goodbye then," said Trevor handing over the money. "And if you're ever in Scotland . . ."

"I'll never be in Scotland," said Douglas. "But thanks all the same." He was about to say something else but decided against it.

"Goodbye," he said. Trevor watched him go, and it was as if part of himself were leaving him, the agony was so great. He looked down at his clenched hands and then sat heavily on a seat. Douglas had disappeared and he would never see him again. He stared at the piece of paper on which was written, he was now sure, his brother's address. He rose slowly to his feet and went to the office and asked which bus he should take to get to the destination he had been assigned by Douglas. He bought a ticket and sat down again and waited.

Nineteen

TREVOR FELT SUDDENLY happy and excited as the bus left, now quite sure that he was on his way to a real destination. Suddenly the small woman who sat in the seat next to him, said,

"I'm going to Ireland at the end of the month. Do you know Ireland?"

"No," said Trevor.

"My daughter and son-in-law are in Belfast," she continued.

"Oh," said Trevor and then with an effort, "What's it like there?"

"He's a joiner and she used to be a secretary. They have a small house. She's just had a baby."

"You must be pleased," said Trevor.

"I am. I am so pleased. But what is there for them over there. Nothing but bombs. It's awful."

"I'm sure it must be terrible," said Trevor.

"Her best friend was shot a year ago. She had a baby and they thought the father was a Protestant activist. They shot her. She opened the door and two masked men shot her just like that."

160

"Are you sure it's safe to go over there then?"

"I have to go. I've been saving up for five years. This is the last time we'll see them."

"Oh I don't know," said Trevor. "You're still young."

She smiled and then said, "But I'm sixty-five, you know. I used to work in a shop here. I'm on my way to see my other daughter."

There was a thought nagging at the back of Trevor's mind. It was to do with the big quarrel he had had with Sheila one night when he had started by saying that her brother-in-law was a waster.

"What about your own brother?" she had said to him.

"What about him?" said Trevor angrily.

"You talk about my brother-in-law but what is your own brother doing? How do you know that he's not a waster?"

"Are you talking about Norman?"

"Who else do you think I'm talking about?"

"Well, remember what you're saying. You were going with him once."

"And why do you think I left him?"

"Why did you?" Trevor shouted almost incoherently.

"Why? I'll tell you why. He said he would marry me but I knew deep down that he wouldn't. He's not the marrying kind."

"And what do you mean by that?"

"Just what I said. He's a waster. I asked him to marry me but he wouldn't. I asked him."

"What did he say?"

"He was drinking as usual. He's bone lazy. All he wanted to do was dress up in his kilt and go to parties."

"Oh shut up," shouted Trevor. "Were you not the same? Did you not want to go to parties too?"

"Maybe. But I also wanted to get married. Your mother . . ."

"What about my mother?"

"She kept both of you under her thumb. She didn't like me because I smoked."

"Are you saying that was why my brother didn't marry you?"

"I don't know. But he would never have married anyway. You have a higher opinion of him than you should have."

The little woman beside him was saying, ". . . and they cut her hair off. She had such beautiful hair too, my daughter was saying. But they cut it all off, and she was left with nothing."

"Is that right?" said Trevor.

"Yes. She's bald now. God knows when her hair will grow again. She had been going with a Protestant, you see. I tell them they should come out here but they won't. They say that Ireland is their home. But what will it be like bringing up a child in Belfast?"

"I don't know," said Trevor.

Again the woman smiled suddenly and said, "Here I am talking about myself and not letting you get a word in edgeways. You're not from Australia, are you?"

"No," said Trevor, "I'm on my way to see my brother. He emigrated here."

"Is that right now? What does he do?"

"I don't know," said Trevor. "We haven't heard from him for over fifteen years."

"Sometimes they go like that. Mary was telling me about a lad from Belfast and they took him home from Canada but he started to drink and couldn't settle down at all. He was

162

home only a year and then he set off for Canada."

So that was what might happen to Norman. Twice he had been told of instances of emigrants who had been brought home and they had gone away again almost as soon as they had arrived in their own country. What use would it be then to buy an air ticket for Norman?

"There are a lot of Irish in Australia," said the woman. "Some of them came out at the time of the Hunger. Still, you never know. Your brother might have done well for himself. My son-in-law is a good husband to my daughter. He's got a steady job as a joiner. He puts the money in my Mary's hand regular every Friday. Well, I'm getting off here. The best of luck to you."

"Thank you," said Trevor. "And the same to you." When the woman had left the bus he sat in his seat thinking.

Had he not admired his brother after all for his sudden wild escape? Was that what was at the root of his respect for him? Had Norman not done what he himself wished to do but didn't have the courage to? That quick, daring leap had impressed him, had it not?

It was like the parable of the Prodigal Son. His brother had been the one who had set off into the blue, fed perhaps among the swine, but hadn't the money to separate himself from his failure. And all the time his brother had been away he himself had looked after his father and mother, and then Sheila. He imagined a field, and Norman walking towards him in the autumn day when the leaves were golden on the ground.

Norman smiled in a superior manner to his older brother who had the spade in his hand. He was laughing, and mocking him. What had Norman not seen in the world outside, what sights had he not known? And he himself had seen and done nothing. Why was it the case that the irresponsible

163

wanderer was always admired and the settled one scorned? It was an injustice, an unfairness. And then even while he himself was being the responsible one his brother had not even sent a Christmas card home. Maybe Douglas was right. Maybe he should forget about him. Was it not more admirable to stay where one was, and was the leap into the unknown a sign more of weakness than of strength?

Suddenly he thought of Sheila and his home with longing. Why had he not written to her or phoned? Maybe she was right and Norman was incapable of facing life or even marrying. He thought of the intricate shadows and darknesses of Scotland and it seemed to him that its old hills and stones and streams and even its rain were infinitely desirable. This country on the other hand was superficial and without echo, its history minimal. The thirst that he felt for his home was so strong that he almost fainted with the joy of it.

And there was the time when his brother had played the record player very loudly when he himself had been studying. Norman used to do that often and when he went and remonstrated with him, Norman would lower the volume for a while and then raise the level again. It had been quite deliberate, a subtle taunting.

There were so many incidents that returned to him, the time that his mother had bought him a new pair of shoes and Norman had insisted on wearing them to a dance without his permission.

And yet again there had been the time when his brother had defended him from that boy whose name he now forgot: and he himself had watched like a girl while the two had fought.

He looked down at the piece of paper which he was clutching sweatily in his hand. What would he find at the end of his journey? Was it possible that his brother was living on his own, like an animal.

"You can keep her," Norman had told him. "The reason I never married her was that she was going with other fellows. One night she told me that she had stayed at home but I found out that she had been with a fellow who worked in the factory. I wasn't sure of her, that was why I never married her." And behind Norman's voice he heard the embittered voice of his mother, "Men! Your father didn't stick to the one woman, I can tell you. He was going with women when he was away from home."

And even now what was Sheila doing while he was away from home? She had said to him before he left, "See that you enjoy yourself," a statement which was entirely uncharacteristic of her. Had she implied that she herself was going to be enjoying herself?

There was no end to the complications of life.

"You're not going to tell me that there aren't some of these girl students that you like?" she would say to him.

"I've told you and told you. I'm not interested. You don't seem to understand what teaching is, that you don't take advantage."

"I know what men are."

"Am I not supposed to speak to them? After all, it's my job. Do you want me to get another job then? I'll do that if you want."

"I don't want you to get another job. But you don't have to be so pally with the students. That girl who's always ringing you, for instance."

"She's doing a PhD. She needs help."

"I know what kind of help she needs."

And what if he did bring his brother home? Would

Norman have to stay with the two of them till he got a job, if he ever did get a job? And was that a good idea? Was it not even possible that Sheila might feel an attraction to him again after his wild wandering life, his stories of a strange world? Might Norman not even deliberately try to set the two of them against each other, as a revenge for his unpayable debt of gratitude?

And would he even like Scotland again? After all he had been used to a mild and sometimes hot climate. Could he settle down in an old country, rainswept most of the time, and cold in the winter. What if he turned on him and said, "I never asked to come home. I didn't want your money or your ticket. I was happy enough where I was. It was you who caused all the trouble."

"Here you are, mate," said the driver. "You get off here."

Trevor hastily left the bus. He was sweating profusely. These little houses, it was in one of them that his brother lived. He passed his handkerchief across his brow, seeing as he did so the marks of the fleas on his arms, marks which were now beginning to lose their raw redness.

He made his way towards the address which he had been given by Douglas.

Twenty

AS HE WAS walking along he was suddenly hit by the thought which came out of the blue and which he blamed himself for not having before. What if his brother was in fact the chief character in Douglas's novel? Perhaps it was Norman who was the child murderer and Douglas had been trying to tell him this all the time. Had he not been giving him all sorts of hints? Was he in fact, by tricking and persecuting Trevor, trying to find background for a new novel?

While thinking these thoughts he found himself standing at the door of a house not unlike Douglas's. He pressed the bell and after a while a young woman came to the door.

"Yes," she said interrogatively.

"My God," though Trevor angrily, "he has deceived me again. Again he has sent me to the wrong house."

"I'm looking for Norman Grierson," he said. The young woman was slim and dark-haired, and wearing a blue shirt which left her arms bare.

"He's not in just now," she said with such a natural air that Trevor was staggered.

"What?" he said idiotically.

"He's not in at the moment," said the woman again, staring at him. "What did you want him for?"

"When will he be home," said Trevor trying to gather himself together.

"He should be home in about half an hour."

Trevor, forgetting that he had no watch, automatically glanced down at the white band on his arm.

"It's half-past four now," said the young woman helpfully. "Did you wish to see him for some particular reason?"

"Excuse me," said Trevor, "but are you, I mean . . . ?"

"I'm his wife if that's what you mean." She was staring at him in a puzzled manner and then said, "If you don't mind my saying so you look like him. I don't suppose . . ."

"I'm his brother," said Trevor. "I'm over from Scotland."

"What?" she said. "His brother. Come in, come in. Why didn't you say so before? He'll be so pleased. He often talks about you. You're the lecturer, aren't you?"

"Yes," said Trevor.

"Well, come in, come in. He'll be so pleased."

Dazedly Trevor allowed himself to be led into the living room.

On the wall a boomerang was hanging with kangaroos painted on the curves. There was a cupboard with glass dishes in it, and in a corner was the inevitable television set. He sat down on one of the two green chairs while the young woman sat opposite him.

"My name's Jean," she said. "I'm a nurse. Norm is working as a groundsman at a local hospital. He's usually back at five o'clock. He's got his own car," she added.

"How did you find him?" she asked.

168

"I'm in Canberra for ten weeks," said Trevor. "A man phoned me up. His name is Douglas."

"Douglas? I don't know him. Perhaps Norm will know him."

"Why did he never write?" said Trevor.

"Oh he's very lazy at writing. We were married ten years ago. We met at the hospital."

"Was he a patient?"

"Yes, he was ill for a while. But he's all right now. He's fine now. I might as well tell you he drank a lot. But he's off it now."

"I heard that from Douglas. He phoned me out of the blue. It was he who gave me the address."

"I'm glad he did. I was always telling Norm to write home but he never did. He hates writing."

"Do you have any children?" said Trevor.

"No, I'm afraid we haven't," and her expression darkened a little. "I'm sure you would like a cup of coffee."

"I wouldn't mind," said Trevor, and she went into the kitchen. On the mantelpiece was a photograph of himself taken when he was perhaps nineteen. He picked it up and looked at it as if it were a picture of someone else. He heard the tap running in the kitchen. So this was where his brother had finally settled, in this small house in this distant part of the world. How strange it all was.

"How is everybody?" Jean shouted from the kitchen. "Norm's father and mother will be dead now, I suppose."

"Yes."

"He used to talk about his mother a lot. I believe she was very strict. She used to tell him to come in earlier at nights. And your own wife, how is she?"

"Sheila? She's fine, thank you."

169

"That's good. And what are you doing out here now then?"

"I'm at the university at Canberra."

"Oh? And when do you go back?"

"In a few days' time."

"Isn't it good that you managed to find us? But he's so lazy at writing. Mind you, he works very hard at his job. He's at his work at eight in the morning. He was lucky to get the job. There's a lot of unemployment here. I suppose you'll know that."

"Yes, I knew that." She came in with a tray on which there were two cups of coffee.

"I was a nurse at the hospital. My parents come from Adelaide. Have you been to Adelaide?"

"No," said Trevor, "but I've heard that it's very pretty."

"Very. But it's very quiet, and very establishment. You know the kind of thing I mean. I left it when I was eighteen."

"I can't get over the fact that he's here," said Trevor. "I mean married and so on. I didn't think that he would be married."

"And why not?"

"I don't know. It didn't occur to me."

"I think sometimes he wants to go on his travels again," said Jean, and Trevor could hear beyond her light laugh another deeper darker voice.

"I imagine so," he said aloud.

Standing on top of the television set was a doll clad in a pink gown, with a black veil over her face. She looked Spanish and airy and eager, perched on tiptoe.

"I was worried that he would be dead," he said.

170

"Dead? Norm? You couldn't kill him off as quickly as that. He's a groundsman at the hospital. I'm on night shift myself so I don't have to go back till eight. He keeps the grounds tidy. He gathers up the leaves and waters the flowers. He's always attending to sprinklers. The land here is very parched, as you will have noticed."

"I've noticed."

"But he'll be so pleased to see you. And I'm so pleased to see you as well. I feel I've always known you. Norm often talks about you."

"Oh?"

"Nothing bad. He said you were a very brilliant scholar. He boasts about you to his friends."

"Does he?"

"He's always boasting about you. Mind you, he doesn't read much himself. He doesn't have the time. We go out sometimes at weekends. There's a club near here we go to, for the company. Norm doesn't drink alcohol, as you can imagine, but he can sit and drink tomato juice."

"He's strong willed then?"

"I'm sure you must know that yourself. In the summer we sometimes go to Adelaide to see my parents."

"Does he like Adelaide?"

"I don't think so, but we go anyway. Are you feeling all right?"

"Yes. It's just that it's all been such a surprise." So he went to visit his parents-in-law while he wouldn't write home to his own parents.

As if Jean had sensed what he was thinking she said, "I have to drag him there, you know. He's a great one for staying in the house. And he's very practical too. He did all the brickwork for the house and he dug up the garden and

171

planted the roses. He watches television a lot.''

She looked at her small watch and said, ''He should be home soon. His job isn't very demanding but it brings us in enough money, especially as I'm working as well. Is your wife working?''

''No,'' said Trevor, and then, ''She has the child to look after. We had the child late.''

As if she hadn't heard him Jean continued, ''He's a very friendly person. He helps the people around here when he can. They all like him.''

''He was always like that,'' said Trevor. ''He was always helpful.''

''He makes friends very easily,'' said Jean proudly. ''Why, if we are ever on a trip he makes friends so quickly, you wouldn't believe it. We were on an excursion in the Murray River direction not so long ago and he made lots of friends. One of them was an old, grey-haired ex-secretary, and he and she used to play the gambling machines. He likes people.''

''He was always like that,'' said Trevor. ''I was shyer.''

''Yes, he said that. He told me that you were shy. Give Trevor his books, he would say, and that's all he wants. It could thunder and storm but Trevor wouldn't be shifted from his books. I believe you were very close, though.''

''Yes,'' said Trevor, ''we were very close. There were just the two of us.''

They sat in silence for a while, neither of them able to think of anything to say, and then Trevor suddenly said,

''Has he ever mentioned anyone called Douglas?''

''Douglas? You referred to him before. No, I don't think he's said anything about anybody with that name.''

''It's just that he phoned me up,'' said Trevor. Why had

172

Douglas lied to him? It wasn't Norman after all who was wandering about Australia: it was Douglas himself.

"I'm sure Norm will know him," she said. "He knows such a lot of people." And then, "It's been quite hard really. You see, he did drink a lot at one time. It took him a long time to get over it. But now that he's stopped I would hate him to have a relapse." It was as if she was trying to give him a subtle warning.

"I certainly wouldn't offer him drink," he said.

"No, it's not that. I'm not worrying about that." Trevor found himself liking Jean.

She seemed unflurried, commonsensical, though he had the feeling that she was anxious and apprehensive about Norman. He found himself comparing the house in which he was sitting to the council flat that he and Norman and their parents had once inhabited.

"I can't stand this place," Norman would say. "I want to get out of here." Their mother didn't want any posters on the walls. And she always complained about the neighbours who played records till all hours. The walls of the house were very thin and all sounds could be clearly heard.

For some reason that he couldn't put into words, Trevor was feeling disappointed. He had expected that his brother, if alive, would be working on a sheep station, or doing some job that was unusual and Australian. The normalcy of the surroundings bothered him, and he wasn't unaware of the pun. Norm. Normalcy. Why, Douglas was more interesting than Norman. Norman hadn't needed to come to Australia to live like this.

The clock on the mantelpiece, which showed two doves whitely intertwined at the top was ticking loudly. He felt uncomfortable in the house, as if he had disturbed a deep silence.

173

Jean was looking more often at her watch. "He should be here any minute now. He would have liked a place nearer at hand but there aren't any. And then these houses aren't very expensive. In Australia you can get help with buying your house. I don't know if you knew that."

"No," said Trevor, "I didn't know."

"Oh yes they're very good that way." She paused and then said, "It wasn't very romantic how we met. One day Norm came up to me in the grounds and said that I reminded him of someone whom he had once known. Who is that, I asked him. My mother, he said. It was lucky for him that he said that. If he had said some other woman, I don't think I would have gone out with him." She was holding her hand in her lap in such a way that Trevor could see the ring. It wasn't nearly as expensive as the one Sheila had. And then it occurred to him rather tardily that Jean was very like Sheila in physical appearance, though she didn't have the Roman nose nor the brooding sexual presence. So it was Sheila and not his mother that Jean had reminded Norman of.

"We went out together for a long time and then I told him that it was time we married. He loves me," she said simply, "but he doesn't know it. Our only sorrow is that we don't have children. Norman is very fond of children. What is your own child like?"

"She is ten years old and very like her mother," said Trevor. "Not at all like me."

"Some day you'll have to bring them," said Jean "We couldn't possibly visit Scotland. We don't have the money."

Twenty-One

———————————

AT THAT MOMENT an old green truck drew up outside the house and Trevor went to the window. He watched the door of the truck opening, and then he saw a naked hairy leg, and then another one. For a moment his brother was standing facing the window at which Trevor was standing before he turned and shut the door of the truck behind him. He was dressed in a pair of white shorts and a blue shirt and he was totally bald. Then he was walking towards the house and Trevor could see his face. He didn't look at all as he did in the photograph taken when he was a soldier in the Argylls. The brow was lined, the face coarse and slightly unshaven: the blue eyes had lost their laughter. The nose looked red as if still registering the days of his drunkenness.

"Are you there, Jean?" he heard his brother say, and then Norman was in the room. For a moment he stared at Trevor without recognizing him, wondering who this stranger was who was in the same room as his wife. Trevor was to remember that blind yet slightly angry gaze for a long time, and then as if a film had been speeded up Norman said,

"Trevor," and then he had rushed forward and embraced

175

his brother. They swayed in each other's arms, while
Norman said over and over, "I don't believe it. Trevor."
Then he pushed him away and said, "Why, you're bald as a
coot. Didn't I tell you, Jean, that our family always became
bald. What are you doing out here?"

Trevor told him and he looked proud and possessive.

"Didn't I tell you, Jean, that he was smart? Well,
woman, haven't you any food for us? I'm working as a
groundsman, did Jean tell you? It's a good job, nothing to it.
When I saw it advertised in the paper I put in for it and they
gave it to me. No worries. They all know Norm is a good
worker. Isn't that right, Jean?"

"Yes," said his wife non-committally, glancing at Trevor
as if wondering how he was taking her husband's chatter.
Husband, thought Trevor, this is her husband, and the word
didn't sound right for Norman.

"I'm telling you I bowled them over at the interview.
Told them I'd been a handyman all over Australia. But I
really like working among growing things, there's nothing
like it."

Trevor expected him to say something about the day he
himself had deliberately lost him in the wood but he didn't
mention it as if he had completely forgotten all about it.

"The ground's a bit parched at the moment but I manage
to get enough water. Fellow from the hospital stopped me
the other day, big surgeon he is, I was telling Jean, and he
said to me, 'Haven't seen the grounds kept so well for years.
How do you do it? So I explained to him what I did and that I
had learned it all back in Bonny Scotland. 'You Scotch?' he
said. 'That's right,' I said, 'Scottish and proud of it.' 'I've
been to Scotland myself,' he said. 'Which part?' I said.
'Edinburgh,' he said. And so we got talking and he told me

176

that he didn't know there was so much work connected with the job. 'We Scots,' I told him, 'we were taught to work hard.' And then he said, 'Thought I'd seen you before.' And I told him, 'Must have been in the wards then. I used to be a patient here.' And then he gave me one look and said 'Which ward?' So I told him I'd been an alcoholic, but I was cured now. 'Well,' he said, 'you Scotch are all the same.' It was Dr Falconer,'' he said turning to his wife. ''That's who it was.''

He stopped suddenly and then said in a different tone, ''I suppose the old people are dead now. I should have written but I never managed it. Many's the time I took the old pen in hand but I never got round to putting anything on paper. The wanderer, that's me,'' he said proudly. ''Did you ever hear of a fellow called Lawson. He could tell you about that.''

For a moment Trevor felt disoriented to hear his brother talking about the poet and story teller. It was exactly the same feeling he had had with Douglas.

''Yes,'' he said, ''they're both dead now. They both died about ten years ago.''

''Is that right? And I never sent a Christmas card. Do you remember the day I left? I told Jean that there was a piper playing me on board. His name was Morrison and he worked in the factory. And there I was standing on the deck keeping a stiff upper lip and you and my mother standing on the quay. By gosh, it was the greatest day of my life. Do you know what I did when I landed? I bought a pony and then I rode all over this great country. One day I came to a farmhouse and this fellow said to me, 'I'd like to go on holiday but I can't get away. Can you do any milking?' 'Milking,' I said, 'of course I can do milking,' though I never could. And do you know he went away with his wife and left me in charge of the

177

farm for a week. And I milked the cows and did all the chores. I used to think about you a lot in those days. You were the one who read all the books. I've never read a book except some stuff by Lawson and Banjo Paterson. Have you heard of Banjo Paterson? He wrote some good stuff. But I told you about the pony, didn't I?''

"Yes," said Trevor, "you wrote home in the early days."

"And then I fell into bad company," he said. Turning towards Jean he called "Is the food ready?"

"You can have it now," said Jean quietly and they all went into the kitchen and sat down at the table.

"Now remember," said Norman, "eat plenty. We have salads here mostly. But today we are having meat." And he piled meat on to his brother's plate. "Jean's got to go at eight."

"I'll go over and see Mary," said Jean. "You two will have plenty to talk about."

"What do you want to see Mary about?"

"She was wondering whether we could baby-sit for her this weekend. Saturday night."

"Right, then," said Norman, and his expression clouded a little.

"You'll stay the night anyway?" said Jean to Trevor.

"If you don't mind: but I'd better be going in the morning. I have to leave Australia in a few days' time. I have packing to do."

He caught the two of them looking at each other significantly and then Norman said briskly, "Eat up, eat up. We can't send you back starved. Eat up. Of course," he said to his wife, "Trevor never used to eat much. He was always buried in his books even at meal times. I remember the nights when he used to read under the bedclothes. And do you remember the time you passed your station in the train because you had been reading? Trevor was always better than me at school, Jean, and one day I had to fight a boy who had been shouting names after him. Isn't that right, Trevor?''

"I remember," said Trevor. Jean looked at him briefly and then turned away.

"We were peasants in those days," said Norman largely. "That's what we were. One day the headmaster took me up to his study and he said to me, 'You were fighting, weren't you?' I was fighting with two other boys who were in a higher class than me and they were cleverer. So he didn't want to belt them. He said to me, 'Hold out your hand, 'and I said, 'I'll take two and no more.' 'We'll see about that,' he said. He gave me two and he told me to hold out the other hand. 'No way,' I said, 'there's a question of fairness here.' 'Fairness?' he said. 'That's right,' I said, 'fairness. What about the two other boys? They're not being punished. Why are they not being punished?' 'It was you who started it,' he said. 'It wasn't me who started it,' I said. 'You're always the troublemaker,' he said. 'No, I'm not,' I said, 'and I'm not taking any more.' And I looked him straight in the face and then he said, 'You get out of here and don't let me see you again.' A few years afterwards I saw him and he was retired and he said to me, 'I remember you. You're Grierson.' But he didn't say any more. I wasn't going to be pushed around by him." He chewed some meat, washing it down with milk, and said, "Same thing happened to me on a site I was working at. This Australian bugger said to me, 'We're paying off some men.' 'Oh?' I said to him just like that (I remember I had a spade in my hand at the time). 'And it looks as if you'll have to go,' he said. Big fat fellow he was. I can still see him. 'What about Macdonald?' I said, 'He came at

179

the same time as me.' This gaffer didn't think I would complain, you see, and he didn't know what to say. 'But just because I'm Scottish,' I said, 'and he's Australian, you're paying me off and not him. That's unfair. There's a question of unfairness here.' And do you know, he didn't say another word. He just walked away. You've got to stand up for yourself in this world or people will trample all over you. Well by gosh I'm glad to see you," he said, leaning over and patting Trevor on the back. "God knows," he said to his wife, "why my mother called him Trevor. It's not a Scottish name. She saw it in a book, I think. Now Norman is a good Scottish name. Plenty of Normans in Scotland. Did I tell you that I learned Maori when I was in New Zealand? Most people don't speak Maori but this night I was playing pool, myself and two other blokes, and a Maori came in and I said to the two blokes, 'I bet you I can speak to this Maori in his own language.' And I did too. They respected me then, you see.''

There was a silence, Trevor unwilling to say something which might explode some hidden mine or other. But Norman was quite prepared to go on.

"There's nothing I hate more than unfairness. I'm not going to have it. There's a doctor in the hospital and he said to me one day, 'One or two people have been complaining about the state of the grounds here.' 'Who are they?' I said. 'Never you mind who they are,' he said to me. 'But I do mind who they are,' I said. And then I said to him, 'Are you complaining?' 'Well,' he said. 'Tell me then,' I said, 'the grounds are in front of you there. You tell me if you're complaining.' 'No,' he said, 'in fairness I can't say that I can complain.' This is good meat, Jean. Where did you get it?''

"In Strachan's.''

"Strachan's. Well, tell him from me next time he's got good meat. If it wasn't for Jean, Trevor, I don't know where I'd be. Used to drink wine all the time. One night I got the DTs. and I saw things crawling about the walls. It took five men to hold me down in the hospital. Then they gave me a jag and I went out like a light. I met Jean and we got married. Don't know what I'd do without her. Do you remember that fellow, what was his name, you know the one who used to go out and attack Catholics, the one who lived beside us? Used to dress very neatly."

"Boyd," said Trevor. "Was it Boyd?"

"That's right, the very fellow, Boyd. He was a Protestant. He used to go out every night and beat up Catholics. And then he used to get beaten up himself. We lived in a council house, Jean, and the Irish would tear up your plants if you tried to have a garden. They were a lot of ruffians. One old lady made a hole in the walls of her room so she could speak to another old lady. Do you remember that, Trevor?" And he burst out laughing. "A big hole in the wall. Well, that was a good meal, Jean." And he pulled his chair back from the table and began to roll a cigarette.

"Smoke, Trevor?"

"No thanks. Not just now."

"Trevor never used to smoke or drink either," Norman said to his wife. "The first time Trevor had a drink, Jean, he was sick all over the lobby, and my mother was mad. I can remember these things so clearly. Now I could take a bottle of whisky a day at one time. But it's a mug's game. Whisky didn't do anyone any good, isn't that right, Jean?" he said watching her clear the things from the table. "Don't stay long at Mary's now. You've got to be at your work at eight. Mary and her husband are Scots, you know," he told Trevor.

"He used to be a policeman somewhere. Where was it, Jean?"

"Before he came out here?"

"No, after."

"I think it was Perth."

"That's right and then they moved here. They have Scottish records and they play them for us sometimes. Andy Stewart, people like that. They're our best friends here. He's a watchman now. He got a job as a watchman."

When it was six o'clock Jean went to see Mary and the two brothers were left alone. Immediately she had gone Trevor said,

"Did you ever meet anyone called Douglas on your travels? A fellow called Malcolm Douglas?"

"Douglas? Douglas? No, I . . ."

"It was him who phoned me up and told me about you. He said he used to be a psychiatric nurse."

"I did meet a fellow called Douglas now that you mention it, back in the early 'seventies. At least I think that was his name. A darkish fellow, is that right?"

"Yes, he's dark-haired."

"He was lodging with me for a while. That was about the time I broke away from the life I was leading. I told him that. I told him I was going to leave and he didn't like it. He was a bit of an oddball. I told him I was going into hospital and he came to see me once or twice. I remember now. He comes from Scotland, or his people do. He heard I was getting married. So he would know about me. And he phoned you up?"

"Yes."

"He was a clever chap that. Always reading books. I had a fight with him once over a drink or something. He had

182

picked up my glass from the counter and he told me that it was his own. I knew that it wasn't. We had a fight and I beat him up. But after that we were friends again. He was a funny fellow, always playing tricks on people. I couldn't make him out at all. One night he accused a pal of mine of being a child murderer: he showed him a photograph from the paper and he looked like him right enough. He used to have blackouts and headaches if it is the same Douglas.''

"That's him all right,'' said Trevor.

All the time his brother was speaking he was thinking, How ordinary he is. He doesn't at all look as I remember him. He used to be handsome, boyish, and adventurous: now he is a bald groundsman.

"And how is Sheila?'' said Norman lightly.

"Oh she's fine.''

"Nice girl that but ambitious. She was too ambitious for me. She was always going on about bettering herself. I got sick of it at the end. Hey, do you remember that time we were in the wood and I shouted to you from behind a tree and you panicked because you thought you were lost? Of course you had no sense of direction. And that other time I tore up your lecture notes. Do you remember that?''

"I remember,'' said Trevor, without trying to correct his interpretation of the incident in the wood.

"The things I've seen since I left you,'' Norman continued. "You wouldn't believe half of them. That fellow Douglas, by the way, nearly ended up in prison. One night they caught him walking along the street with a brick in his hand. He was going to break into a shop or a warehouse or something. But they let him off for lack of evidence. He was a smooth talker, right enough.''

"It was he who had the brick?''

"Yes, but I'll tell you something else about Sheila. I knew she was going with other people when I was in the Army. A mate of mine told me about her. But she's a nice girl. I nearly sent you a present from Australia but I didn't have any money. I never had any money. I used to live in dosshouses, you know. Then one night I said to myself, 'This has got to stop', and I put myself into the hospital, and I've never looked back since. Tell me something. What did mother die of?"

"Heart," said Trevor. "She was living with us."

"That was very good of you to take her in, and it makes me feel ashamed. But the thing was, with me it was always come-day go-day. You know that. Do you remember the night there was thunder and lightning? My mother nearly had a fit and I was cycling home from Arrochar? It was one in the morning when I got home."

"Yes, she was walking up and down in her dressing gown all night."

"I can imagine. Well, those were the good old days. I think of them a lot. I had a record player at one time but I never listen to records now except when we visit Mary and Teddy. I bet you were surprised when that fellow phoned you. Many's the time I helped him out. One night when he didn't have any money I took him to my digs. It was an old woman who was the landlady. She had been a matron in the First World War and had tons of medals. Nice old lady that."

While Norman was talking Trevor was looking about the room, and noticed for the first time that there were hardly any ornaments, and only the bare minimum of furniture. He couldn't understand why Jean had married his brother. And then for some reason he remembered himself and Norman

184

carrying upstairs into their council flat a wardrobe which their mother had bought in Grants. They were puffing and panting and Norman was saying, "This wardrobe is far too heavy. One of these days I'll have furniture and it will be much lighter than this." He saw again the window on the first floor landing and the clothes hanging out on the line and it seemed to him that his heart was breaking with the pity of it all. He saw some of his own socks and some of Norman's swaying in the wind on the clothes-line on a spring day. The contrast between the greenness of home and the drought of Australia came to him like a blow under the heart.

"I have a patch of vegetables at the back," said Norman. "I do quite a bit of digging. Do you remember when we moved into that council house? It was me who planted the flowers. I was very keen on flowers, only the Irish dug them up again. You didn't want to have anything to do with the garden: and you didn't want to tackle the Irish but I went to the house of one of them, big fellow he was, and I said he had better cut it out. He was very nice and gave me a cup of tea. The things that come back to you. He was a big fellow and he was standing at the sink shaving at the time, in his singlet. He could have cut me in half: O'Reilly his name was, I think. And then there was the time when the people below were playing their radiogram till all hours. The police wouldn't do anything about it and they were bothering us all the time so I went down and sorted them. All these things come back to you. Sometimes when I can't sleep — I don't sleep so well since I gave up the drink — I lie in my bed thinking and all sorts of things come back to me. There was the time at your wedding before I left and you came up to me with tears in your eyes and you said, 'I'm sorry, Norman.' You said that over and over and you could hardly stand on your feet. And I kept saying, 'It's all right, it's all right.' And you went on and on, 'It's not all right at all. It's far from all right. Are you sure you don't mind?' you kept saying. And I was laughing because I'd never seen you so drunk before. It's strange how you remember these things.''

All the time that Norman was speaking Trevor felt sleepy and almost as if he were dreaming.

Suddenly he said, "Do you have a phone here?"

"A phone? No, we don't have the phone."

"Oh?"

"But there's a phone box down the road if you want."

"No, it's all right."

"If it was anything urgent?"

"No, it isn't urgent," said Trevor, trying to control his voice. "It's not at all urgent." He felt as if he were about to scream, a loud howl against reality.

And so they talked about this and that till the time came for him to go to bed. Jean, of course, was sleeping at the hospital.

"We have a small room," said Norman. "I suppose you could call it a guest room," he added wryly. And he showed Trevor into a tiny room whose wardrobe was overflowing with clothes.

"I can never manage to shut the door of this wardrobe properly," he said. "One of these days I'll get round to it. I hope you'll sleep all right. If you hear anyone moving about at night it'll be me. I make cups of coffee for myself."

"That's all right," said Trevor, and Norman looked at him affectionately as if he couldn't believe that he was there. When Norman had left the room Trevor undressed slowly, seeing through the window a large, round, white moon swimming in the blue of the sky. He imagined it shining above the tenements of Glasgow creating out of that poverty and blackness a spurious brilliance of its own. Soon he would have to leave, and take the plane home and he found that he was already looking forward to the journey.

Everything had come full circle, his brother was safe, he was not buried in a wilderness underneath an alien moon. And Trevor felt such piercing sorrow because of it. And yet why should he feel sorrow? Why should he not feel happy that his brother was living under a roof, with a job, and married? He couldn't understand what was wrong with him.

As Norman had warned him, he heard movements in the middle of the night, footsteps and the running of water. On the table he found a letter which said that Norman was late with his subscription for the *Scottish Field*. After an hour or so he fell asleep.

When he woke the sun was shining through the flimsy curtains and he felt happy to be leaving, as if he had successfully completed a necessary duty. Over breakfast the two of them didn't speak much. When they had finished Trevor said, "Well, I'd better be moving off."

"I suppose so," said Norman. "You'll excuse me if I don't go to the bus with you."

They stared at each other for a long time as if across the waste of the years and then Trevor was walking away from the house with his case in his hand. He climbed on to the bus, thought of Glasgow, and was happy. He didn't wish to have anything more to do with the tangle of the past: it was as if he had been purified of it. And yet without his willing it a picture came into his mind of the two of them in the wood. Was it his brother who had hidden, or was it himself? He couldn't remember. More than anything in the world he wished to phone Sheila, hear her voice across the miles that separated them. It was as if an iron cloak of responsibility had settled on him, as if he could apply to himself the word "husband" which somehow he had not been able to do before. A woman standing in front of a house threw a basin of water across her lawn and in its full transparent curve he saw a wasteful, vulnerable beauty and recklessness that overwhelmed him with thoughts which were both heavy and joyful at the same time.

"I'm going home," he thought, "I'm going home."

Twenty-Two

THAT NIGHT WHEN Jean came home from work she was very angry.

"I'm afraid I didn't like your brother much," she said between pursed lips. "He was examining the house as if he didn't think much of it. I saw him trying to see if there were any ornaments."

"Not Trevor," said Norman defensively. "Not Trevor. All he's interested in is books."

"Don't you believe it. He didn't say much, did he? He was weighing everything up. You shouldn't have gone on so much about your drink problem. You come out with everything like a child."

"He had to know. I couldn't offer him a drink, could I?"

"He didn't need a drink. And what about that Sheila you were going with? I noticed you didn't say anything about her. He was always the favoured one, you said. If he ever came here you would tell him so, you said. But you're as weak as water. He was laughing at you all the time, with all your talk of that doctor who had told you that you were doing a good job as a groundsman. What do you think

189

people like your brother think of groundsmen? Anyone would think you ran the hospital, the way you were talking. What would a college lecturer think of a groundsman? You're always so open.''

Norman thought: This was the way Sheila used to go on, accusing him of lack of ambition.

''You're probably right,'' he said, ''but then he's my brother after all.''

''What sort of brother is he? He never sent you money when you needed it. He could have. He's got a big salary. Why couldn't he have sent you money?''

''I'm happy now,'' said Norman pacifically.

''That's what you say. If you're so happy why can't you sleep at nights? And it was me who had to propose to you. You don't care about me at all, making me a laughing stock in front of all these people. Did he say anything about the room?''

''No. He said that he had a good sleep.''

''And I don't suppose you locked the door so that he couldn't see all those old clothes in the wardrobe. I don't understand you. Anyway it's nothing to do with me. He's your brother.''

''Yes,'' said Norman firmly. ''He's my brother.'' And he left the room and went outside and began furiously to clip the hedge. After a while Jean came out, looked at him, and then went over and put her arms around his neck.

''I'm a bitch, isn't that what you're thinking?''

''No,'' said Norman, ''I'm thinking how lucky I am.''

Twenty-Three

———————

TREVOR HEARD THE voice of the stewardess telling them to fasten their safety belts. In a short while they would be landing at Glasgow Airport. But all around them at the moment was a map of clouds, like mound upon mound of snow. But at least it was better than that solid wall of heat that had met them at Colombo so that he had to fan himself with the magazine he was reading. The Italian woman who had moved continually in front of the screen while the film was being shown, who had taken her child on perpetual visits to the lavatory, and talked to it so loudly that the commentary could not be heard, was asleep, her mouth open. He looked out of the window and far below he could see green fields and threads of rivers. The houses and cars were like toys in a miniature kingdom. How strange it was that he should ache so much for home, for its emerald greenness and its crowded, rainswept tenements. The plane shuddered to a halt and he was walking along the passageway with his case. The stewardess standing at the door, said "Thank you, sir."

"Thank you," he said automatically. He waited at the revolving ring of cases and then strode along the green corridor which said NOTHING TO DECLARE. He didn't see Sheila and Carol at first and then he did. And then they were all clasped in each other's arms and walking out into the rain which was falling on Glasgow Airport.

"Shall I tell her?" he wondered as they sat close together in the taxi.

She was staring at him with a hurt, wondering look but she didn't speak. This time it will begin again, he thought, but it will be different. Carol was stretching out her hands for the koala bear that he was holding. Its open, laughing face with the small beady eyes was smiling at her. Its button nose made it seem cuddly and affectionate. Her hands were held out greedily and impatiently for it. He smiled at his wife.